I0636757

THE SWEET SPOT

Wisdom Editions
Minneapolis

SECOND CALUMET EDITION DECEMBER 2022
The Sweet Spot: Where Business Strategy, Positive Psychology and
Faith Principles Converge.

Copyright © 2022 by Mike Ferrell. All rights reserved.

No part of this book may be used or reproduced in any manner
whatsoever without written permission except in the case of brief
quotations used in critical articles and reviews. For information,
write to Calumet Editions, 6800 France Ave. S., Suite 370,

Minneapolis, MN 55435

10 9 8 7 6 5 4 3 2
ISBN: 978-1-959770-47-3

Cover and interior design: Gary Lindberg

principledflourishing.com

THE SWEET SPOT

WHERE BUSINESS STRATEGY, POSITIVE PSYCHOLOGY AND FAITH PRINCIPLES CONVERGE

Mike Ferrell

Wisdom Editions

Minneapolis

Table of Contents

Dedicated to my mom, without whose insistence
from above this book would not have been a reality!

Also by
Mike Ferrell

Ultimate Breakthrough Planning:
The Business Funnel Approach

Sell Like a Monk:
Timeless "Rules" for Modern Selling

Foreword

In 2018, I got a phone call from a person that said they would like to have a cup of coffee. The gentleman was an entrepreneur looking to dig deeper into the integration of faith and work. I knew before our first cup of coffee was finished that there would be many more cups to follow. We shared a common vision and passion for inspiring and forming a new generation of business leaders who value people over profits and find profit as the fruit of providing goods and services that are truly good and truly serve.

Since that day, it's been a privilege to work with Mike to cast a vision together for how it is that we can help businesses flourish by helping people flourish. Mike's extensive experience as an entrepreneur, executive coach, and business leader, combined with his latest work with the Benedictine Leadership Institute at Mount Marty University, has inspired a holistic vision for business success by combining timeless leadership principles with modern business practices.

I've been privileged to watch Mike work as we built a program of Integrated Leadership at Mount Marty. I've observed his dedicated focus and practical vision for equipping professional leaders with the tools necessary to live well and lead well. We live in extraordinary times. Not unlike the time of the great monk Benedict of Nursia. Social institutions like family, education, politics and business seem to be corroded, corrupted or collapsing as they go through soul-searching moments in modern times. I believe that with *The Sweet Spot*, Mike has a vision and a plan to help individuals address the nature and purpose of business and how it is that business leaders can seek to form integrated cultures founded upon timeless principles of faith, lived out in habits of virtue, that create healthy and productive businesses that flourish not just when times are good, but most especially when crises are encountered.

This book will be one that all business leaders will want to consult as we consider what the new reality will be for businesses in a post-pandemic world. What is the nature of the purpose of business? Can business be a force for good? What does excellence in business look like, and how can it be achieved? Are faith principles compatible with a successful business strategy? How does the development of positive psychology and personal character impact how we do business? Mike addresses these questions and so many more in the coming pages of this great book. I think you will gain new insights about how to live and flourish personally and professionally, and I'm not sure if it will help you hit a hole in one, but certainly, you'll find *The Sweet Spot* and the feeling that comes with knowing you were able to bring it all together.

Joe Rutten, Director
Benedictine Leadership Institute
Mount Marty University
Yankton, SD

Executive Director
Catholic Men's Business Fraternity
Sioux Falls, SD

Introduction

The Crash of 2008

On Monday morning, September 15, 2008, I was working with sixteen insurance brokerage companies, thirty-five community banks, and dozens of financial advisors throughout the country. At 6:15 a.m., I left Minneapolis and flew to Charlotte, North Carolina, and had just landed at the airport. As I walked through the terminal, I could see people gathered around TV screens watching the news. Suddenly my Blackberry started going off, messages from clients all over the country wanting to speak with me. It had just been announced that Lehman Bros. had filed for bankruptcy, and it was the onset of the worst financial crisis since the Great Depression.

In the early days of that crisis, I spent most of my time talking to clients about what they needed to focus on to keep moving forward. There was a sense of panic in the industry, and it was all I could do to try and keep some sanity with my clients. While I was doing this, I also had that thought creeping in the back of my mind that if this crisis kept going, my own business was going to face a major challenge.

Over the next two years, I kept this balancing act, keeping a positive outlook with clients while privately brooding over my business and my work. In 2012, the financial crisis finally took its toll on me. Many of my clients had either gone out of business, merged or consolidated, and my client list was dwindling. I had tried to diversify my business based on my book *Ultimate Breakthrough Planning*, and it had allowed me to move into other industries, and that move, though relatively successful, was stretching me thin and burning me out.

By the end of that year, I was starting to do things that were completely against what I had stood for, and I was making bad decisions based on survival. In 2013, I went through a divorce and lost much of what I had spent so long building up. Not only that, but I also lost my purpose and my confidence, and the culmination of these things would take me to some very dark places over the next two years.

In 2015, I decided to leave the Twin Cities, where I had been for thirty-three years, and go back to where I had grown up in South Dakota. I would begin to rebuild what I had worked for, but the process was extremely slow. In addition, I was now working with clients in areas that I was not committed to, and the quality of my work and service was average at best. About that time, I began to deeply reflect on my life, my purpose, and what had transpired over the past six years. I began to ask questions about what it was that had allowed some of my clients in the early days of the financial crisis to rise above the chaos and survive and thrive while others did not survive and took many folks down with them.

A Tale of Four Friends

I recently got together with three longtime friends of mine. The four of us had not been together in over twenty-five years, but within fifteen minutes of meeting, it was just like old times. We spent time catching up with each other's lives, families, work and health (since we're all getting older), and it was interesting to listen to everyone's stories. Through the course of those conversations, one of my friends was talking about his work. He has been with the same company for thirty-two years and is the second-longest tenured person at the company. He has risen through the ranks and is one of the top executives. So far, the story sounds pretty good; however, he also said that when he wakes up on Sunday mornings, he starts to get sick to his stomach because he knows he has to go back to work in less than twenty-four hours. Wow! Here's one of the top executives of the company, and he does not want to go to work on Monday morning. He also explained that the company had been bought and sold a couple of times and that it just wasn't the same place it used to be. That got me thinking about what it was about that company that caused him to feel that way, and if he feels that way, I wonder how many other of the sixty employees feel the same way?

Another of our friends is a salesman. He had been working for a company for almost thirty years, and the company had been bought and sold numerous times. But through it all, he remained loyal to them and had been one of the company's top salespeople. But recently, he had a new director of sales, and that person apparently decided that he could get the same results by paying someone less experienced, less money, and so they let my friend go. After thirty years and still an outstanding performer, he was unceremoniously dumped. Again, I thought about the belief systems and purpose of that company. Is their purpose solely to make money without any thought about the individuals' backs they are making it on?

My third friend has worked for a company for only a few years, leading his division to outstanding results. His boss mostly leaves him alone and lets him do what he needs to do to keep growing his revenue. However, now they are talking about an expansion, and his initial reaction is to wonder will they continue to let him do what's been successful or, because of the expansion, will they start breathing down his back for bigger results?

As I reflected on my friends and their situations, I thought about how their situations may be different if the companies they worked for had a different approach to the way they treat their people and the purpose they have for their companies. Over the years, I've often asked clients about the soul of their company and usually get a confused look, meaning, "what is your company all about?" Is it just to sell products and services that make the owner, shareholders or directors rich, or is it about a much bigger purpose, a higher purpose where everyone enjoys success? There are some telling statistics on how companies and small businesses are doing. For example, in a 2015 survey by Gallup, 68 percent of all employees are either not engaged or actively disengaged in their jobs. That's over two-thirds of the people that work today are not engaged in their jobs. This glaring statistic should make all businesses take a look inside and determine if they truly are working for a higher good.

Why I Wrote This Book

I'm an avid golfer, and when a golfer hits a golf shot square, right on the face of the club, there is a feeling on that shot that you know you hit it perfectly. It creates a sound and a feel that golfers typically refer to as the "sweet spot."

I decided to write this book because I felt that over nearly forty years of the journey that I've traveled, there had been times in my life and my business when everything seemed to come together perfectly, in other words, the "sweet spot." As I've examined and reflected on this journey that I've been on and especially the difficult times of the financial crisis of 2008 and the stories from my three friends, I found that those businesses and organizations I've worked with had three things in harmony and these three things helped them stay the course through good times and difficult times. Those three things are sound strategy, positive psychology and faith principles.

The first area is what I call the foundation; it's faith principles. I'm not talking about a particular religion or a particular belief, but when I refer to faith, I refer to the understanding of a higher power and how that higher power works in your life. How does faith come into play in your work, business and organization? And what exactly should it look like and feel like? I'm Catholic; however, it is not my intent to shove Catholic teaching down your throat. However, I do believe there are specific faith principles when used as the foundation that can lead to successful and flourishing organizations.

The second area is positive psychology, and this area is all about your belief in the success of what you are doing and focusing on the things that make people happy. The study of this type of psychology started with Martin Seligman's work and the development of positive psychology. There are hundreds of teachers, writers, speakers, and leaders in this area, including Napoleon Hill, Zig Zigler, Tony Robbins, Jack Canfield, Mark Victor Hansen, T. Harv Ecker and many others. It's important to note that we're not just talking about "feel good" work but actual science, science that has been studied and tested empirically to understand the "how" of happiness. The basis of that science is philosophy and theology and the study of virtue. Positive psychology is the science of virtue. It starts with a positive approach and a belief that there is abundance in this world, and you deserve it and are grateful for it. You deserve success. But when I write about this area, I'm not going to spend a lot of time going over what they have already taught. As a student of many of them, I strongly believe in their teachings. What I'm more interested in is the relationship between positive psychology and how it relates to business strategy and faith principles.

The third area is business strategy itself and how it interrelates with the other two. I've already written one book on business strategy, and it's not my intent to rehash what I've already written about. Instead, I want to look at specific strategies that work well with faith principles and positive psychology and how the three might look together.

Now, as you read this, you may be thinking about who this book is really for, so let me answer that question. This book is for anyone who owns a business, anyone who runs a business, anyone that manages a group of people, anyone who leads an organization, and especially anyone that is feeling like they're just not sure how to get to the point in their work lives where things are firing on all cylinders.

In the following chapters, I will examine the three areas above and how they can all work in unison to create a business, company or organization that functions profitably, with dignity, and with an emphasis on the human person and a higher good.

Today we live in a world ripe with cynicism, conflict and hatred. It's men against women, religion against religion, Democrats against Republicans, good against evil. We also live in a world where many people have checked out as a result of all this negativity. As a business owner and leader, that is the hand we're dealt. My lofty goal in this book is to give you ideas to change that hand you've been dealt and rebuild the narrative about your work, your business and your organization that get people engaged and make you more successful while being confident you're living and working well.

One More Thing

When I wrote *Ultimate Breakthrough Planning*, I wrote it as a simple tool for businesses and organizations to use for strategic planning. This book has the same goal, to be a basic primer and tool that can give leaders of organizations and teams principles and tools to help them survive and flourish in normal times and during turbulent times. This is not an academic text, and you don't need to read it from front to back. Go to the chapters that interest you, and hopefully, if I've done my job, you can pick out principles and strategies you can put to work immediately. I've also included a list of resources I've used and recommended in writing this book if you would like to do a deeper dive. I am not a scholar, I am not clergy, I am not overly degreed, I don't consider myself a particular expert on anything; what I am is an observer and practitioner.

In my journey through life, business and faith as a leader, consultant, advisor, coach and entrepreneur, I have observed what has worked in organizations and what has not worked. I have been blessed with success in some of my ventures. I have also been blessed with miserable failures in others, and in those failures have tried to learn lessons that would be beneficial in the future. My faith journey has had ebbs and flows like most, times when I felt deeply connected to my faith and times when it was very distant. I have been blessed by the fact that my faith has come full circle, and now it is connected to my work. That is the prelude from where this, my third book, comes from.

As I write the final edits to this book, the world has turned upside down from a global pandemic called the coronavirus. Financial markets have crashed, and life as we knew it has ground to a halt. I write this part of the book while self-quarantining in my home office. Little did I know when I wrote this book the last financial crisis's reflections would be so prominent today. And as this revised edition comes out, we can add war in Europe to the crisis environment as well. Though the challenges are somewhat different and the circumstances different, many of the principles I lay out in the following chapters will directly correlate with what we are going through now. I hope that some of those lessons will help you and your organization weather this storm. I also welcome your input; feel free to visit my website www. principledflourishing.com for more tools and ideas and to connect with me.

CHAPTER 1
Purpose: The Soul of Business

I want to discuss why a company exists in the first place. In other words, why are we here? I think many people assume, wrongly, that a company exists simply to make money. While this is an important result of the company's existence, we have to go deeper and find the real reasons for our being... Purpose (which should last at least 100 years) should not be confused with specific goals or business strategies (which should change many times in 100 years). Whereas you might achieve a goal or complete a strategy, you cannot fulfill a purpose; it's like a guiding star on the horizon forever pursued but never reached. Yet although purpose itself does not change, it does inspire change. The very fact that purpose can never be fully realized means that an organization can never stop stimulating change and progress.

—David Packard, in a 1960 speech to Hewlett Packard's training division.

Why Do You Do What You Do?

In 2008, I wrote my first book *Ultimate Breakthrough Planning: The Business Funnel Approach*. In it, I laid out a process for strategic planning that encompassed six areas of business strategy. Those areas, vision and mission, leadership, sales process, marketing systems, customer service, and strategic alliances, were areas of strategy that, in my experience, were critical to the success of a business. However, shortly after writing the book, the world took a dark turn, the financial crisis that struck tested businesses all over the world in unprecedented ways. The economy crashed, a recession hit, and people lost billions of dollars in the equity of their homes and the value of their retirement and investment accounts.

As I worked with businesses through this darkness, it became very clear that some of them were much less affected by the crisis than others. As I reflected back on that a few years later, I wondered what helped them weather the storm and, in some cases, even thrive during one of the most difficult economic times in our country. One of the very first things that came to mind was that many of the clients who survived and thrived had taken the step to clearly define why they were here and what their purpose was on the strategy that would help them achieve their goals. In addition, it gets leadership, employees and communities aligned in the right direction. Purpose also guides the culture of the organization and how it treats all stakeholders. It provides a framework for decision-making as well as a moral and ethical compass. I had two very distinctly different clients when it came to purpose. The first client completely understood their purpose. They existed to help people live financially secure in retirement, and everything they did was built around that purpose. The other client was a second generation client whose sole purpose was to take as much from the business as possible to create the lifestyle he wanted. His employees knew very well what that meant; it meant they were to cut corners and keep costs down so my client could take home more income. I'm sure you can see by now which client survived and even thrived during the financial crisis and which one would not survive it.

Why is Purpose Important?

Purpose gives an organization soul, and an organization functioning with a purpose also has some very real positive results. There is also a clear understanding now in the business world that purpose is very important. In a study by Quartz Insights, they found some very interesting results:

1. 64 percent of the CEOs who responded to their survey believe that brands, rather than governments, are primarily responsible for driving social change.

2. 73 percent said purposeful leadership would become as important as financial performance.

3. 65 percent think current social and political trends are pushing leaders to define their purpose and demanding that organizations take a stand.

In another study by Accenture, it was found that 64 percent of companies that have a stated purpose showed positive growth, while 42 percent that didn't have a purpose showed growth. And maybe the most telling statistic, in the past three years, 58 percent of companies that had a clearly articulated and understood purpose showed a 10 percent or greater growth rate versus 42 percent that didn't have a defined purpose. Having purpose not only makes sense, but it is also profitable.

In 2019 at the Business Roundtable, two hundred CEOs released a joint statement affirming these points:

1. The Business Roundtable, a group of chief executive officers of nearly two hundred major US corporations, issues a statement with a new definition of the "purpose of a corporation."

2. The reimagined idea of a corporation drops the age-old notion that they function first and foremost to serve their shareholders and maximize profits.

3. Investing in employees, delivering value to customers, dealing ethically with suppliers, and supporting outside communities are now at the forefront of American business goals. (Source: CNBC, August 19, 2019.)

It was the first time this group of CEOs shifted from shareholder value to stakeholder commitment. In January of 2020, at the Davos World Economic Forum, these points were also brought forth. Purpose is now the trending idea for businesses and organizations all over the world, but there is also a key result of purpose, and that is employee engagement. The statistics bear out that organizations with a clear purpose that is communicated and acted upon outperform their competitors that don't, and they also have a higher employee satisfaction rate than those organizations that don't have a clear purpose.

Employees today want more than just a paycheck and benefits. They want to feel like they are part of something and are motivated by working toward some purpose. According to the Gallup Organization, almost 70 percent of employees today are either disengaged or actively disengaged in their work, think of the toll that is taking on the productivity of the organization. Those companies that have a clear purpose and understand their "why" have a clear advantage when it comes to engaging and motivating their employees. And that leads to higher productivity, better customer satisfaction, and ultimately more profitability.

It's also important to note that it's not just big corporations that are looking at this idea of purpose. Many small businesses that have started over the past few years have directly connected their purpose to what they do. They clearly state their purpose and incorporate it into how they interact with all stakeholders. The client mentioned earlier made sure that all his employees clearly understood why the business existed, as did their clients and vendors, and the purpose was constantly part of the business's culture.

The COVID pandemic also brought with it an entirely different set of issues to deal with and those companies that were able to stand their ground on their purpose have survived and sometimes lived through it.

The Golden Circle

Simon Sinek is one of the leading experts on purpose. In his book, *Start With Why*, he undertakes the topic of purpose and why it's important. In the book and in his famous TED talk called "The Golden Circle," he talks about how unique organizations, such as Apple, look at the "What," "How" and "Why" they do things from the inside out, not the outside in like most organizations. He says, "The Golden Circle is an alternative perspective to existing assumptions about why some leaders and organizations have achieved such a disproportionate degree of influence. It offers clear insight as to how Apple is able to innovate in so many diverse industries and never lose its ability to do so. It explains why people tattoo Harley-Davidson logos on their bodies. It provides a clear understanding not just of how Southwest Airlines created the most profitable airline in history but why the things it did worked. It even gives some clarity as to why people followed Dr. Martin Luther King Jr. in a movement that changed a nation and why we took up John F. Kennedy's challenge to put a man on the moon even after he died. The Golden Circle shows how these leaders were able to inspire action instead of manipulating people to act."

Understanding The Golden Circle first requires that we understand each part of the circle. The outer layer is the "What." This is what an organization does and is typically the easiest one for organizations to define. The second layer is the "How." Here, organizations may have a value proposition, unique selling proposition or how they explain their differentiation from other organizations. The innermost circle is the "Why." Very few organizations can clearly articulate this. Here, we look at purpose, cause and belief. The majority of companies and organizations function from the outside in, defining their what and how but never really getting to their why. The truly innovative companies and organizations clearly define their purpose or their "why" and then work from the inside out. Everything is based on the "why" first.

Finding Your Purpose

Before you find your purpose, it's important to distinguish between what is purpose versus mission, vision and guiding principles (values). Many organizations have created mission statements or have a list of values on their walls, but in not understanding and stating their purpose, they are missing the initial step. Oftentimes I have seen purpose confused with vision, mission and values. All of these are important, but purpose is the reason for being—the overall "northstar" that aligns with the other organizational statements. Everything should revolve around purpose; mission is the actual purpose in action, and guiding principles or values can be the "how" it will be achieved. We'll discuss those in the next section.

So how does an organization find its purpose? Here are some basic steps that can help you and your organization start to define your purpose. It's important to note here that stating your purpose is just the beginning; you must incorporate that purpose into your organization's DNA for it to be lived out. The biggest reason for failure to incorporate purpose is superficiality, so it must be acted upon.

1. Ask the question, why do we exist? What is the reason the organization exists, and how do our goods and services impact why we exist?

2. Get input from stakeholders, including management, employees, customers, vendors and the community.

3. Communicating your purpose to all members of the organization and then creating a plan that gets everyone involved in the implementation of your defined purpose.

4. Create a story and action with your brand; it's not just about what you say and do but how you say it and do it.

5. Activate and build a movement, this step takes the longest, but it happens when everyone is on the same page, telling the same story and committed to the purpose.

Integrating Purpose into the Organization: Vision, Mission, Guiding Principles

Once you understand your purpose, then you must put it into action. To do this, you must determine your vision, mission and guiding principles. Let's define these:

Vision: This is looking forward. What does your organization look like in the future? It's hard to get to where you're going if you don't know your destination. Vision represents future purpose, providing a picture of what the organization is working toward.

Mission: A mission is a clear, concise statement that represents the purpose put into action. It's the "what" we do. The mission sets the purpose in action so that it can be executed.

Guiding Beliefs: Sometimes, these are called values; however, I believe that guiding beliefs or principles better explain the "how" we do things. These are the bedrocks on how we will execute the mission and vision.

Let's take a deeper look into these three areas because they sometimes are relegated to posters on the wall, and they need to be embedded into the culture of the organization.

Vision

Vision is the road map; it's where you want to go. And it's important that vision has two focuses: inward- and outward-looking. The inward-looking vision is always examining who we are and making sure that who we are can get us to the outward vision. The outward vision is our goals and what we want to achieve. I had a client several years ago who had a clear outward vision of wanting to become the largest company in his industry and region. However, he didn't do an inward look at how he was structured, and as I looked at his structure, it was very clear that he wasn't set up to become the largest and, in fact, had he gone down the path, it would have been disastrous. In the Benedictine tradition, the outward vision is to serve and praise God. The inward vision is the specific process that they do, which I'll talk about more in a later chapter.

Mission

Understanding what we do is pretty common in most organizations. Where you get the disconnect is when what you do becomes secondary to how you're doing things. Here's an example: during the financial crisis, there were many financial services companies who said what they did was manage a client's money for growth. However, as the market crashed, they began to do questionable practices to try and keep the clients happy. As clients began to figure out what they were doing, they realized it was just the opposite of what they said they were doing, and they began to bail like rats off a sinking ship. It's also important to note that sometimes the mission changes based on the environment. There was no playbook for COVID-19, and as businesses tried to figure out how to navigate those waters, many had to re-think what their real mission was and how to make that happen. Restaurants were especially challenged to carry out their mission, if the mission had anything to do with a dining experience, that had to change course because the restaurant was closed to inside dining, so they had to redefine what dining experience meant. Many didn't make it, but others figured out different methods of creating a dining experience through take-out dining.

Guiding Beliefs

The guiding beliefs are those things that we value most in how we do things and how we interact with all stakeholders. Many organizations call these values, but I think guiding beliefs more adeptly describe the "how" we do things and what is most important to us as an organization. These guiding beliefs dictate how we operate day to day in everything we do. They help us as a compass helps keep us on track toward our vision and carrying out our mission and purpose. It's one of the first things I look for when visiting a potential client's business or organization. Are these guiding beliefs visible, and are they being carried out? In many cases, I'll find out what those guiding beliefs are before I meet with the client, and then in the interview process, I can ask direct questions about how those guiding beliefs are being executed. There have been some instances where the principal of the business said one thing, but as I visited with employees, it became very apparent that there were two different things being done and said. It doesn't take long to figure out what's really happening if you just observe what's going on.

The Pursuit of Higher Purpose

When we talk about higher purpose, we're taking the whole idea of purpose and turning it up a notch. The pursuit of higher purpose comes about when the defined purpose has something to do with a higher good. When a business does something not only for profit but also for a greater good, then we bring in the idea of higher purpose. In Robert Quinn's book, *The Pursuit of Higher Purpose*, he defines higher purpose as "higher purpose is a prosocial goal that is defined not in terms of economic output but in terms of the contribution that the organization makes to society." One distinction that needs to be made here, though, is this is not some sudden wokeness that the organization has jumped on the bandwagon because of pressure from external sources. Unfortunately, in today's environment, many businesses and organizations have made knee-jerk decisions to become woke simply because it's the popular thing to do. It becomes very transparent to see through when companies are doing this, and this is not a higher purpose.

This being said when the pursuit of higher purpose is done with intent to a prosocial commitment it can be very powerful and very profitable. Just because you are pursuing a higher purpose does not mean you can't make money. I have had clients over the years that were pursuing higher purpose and they didn't really even know what they were doing. I can remember one in particular that committed a percent of profits to a charitable organization. The first thing he did was to connect everyone in the organization so that everyone knows what that charitable organization did and how it impacted the lives of the people that it helped. He also incorporated his vision of his business to include the support of the charitable organizations so that everyone understood his position. The business was very successful and the employees went above and beyond to make it successful because they knew the more successful it was the more they were supporting the charitable organization. This is an example of pursuing a higher purpose and it can be a very powerful pursuit.

Once we understand these principles, we can begin to understand how we integrate purpose into the organization. Phil Sotok of DPMC USA works with large corporations on purpose and integrating it into organizations. In an article called *The Purpose Revolution*, he talks about what purpose is not and then how to integrate it into the organization. First, purpose is not strategy; it is not another tactic to be used by management. Second, purpose is not profit; it can lead to profit but is not profit in and of itself. Third, purpose is not PR; it's not some fancy phrase or tagline that is used in marketing. Fourth, purpose is not a one-way street; in other words, it's not a top-down approach but a top-down and bottom-up approach. Fifth, purpose is not passive; it's not something that is just decided upon and then put in a drawer. Everything the organization does must revolve around it. Sotok goes on to discuss seven characteristics that internalize purpose.

1. Knowledge that a purpose exists and the ability of team members to explain it in their own words.

2. Understanding its importance and relevance to the point the people know how it relates to them.

3. Visible commitment to the purpose that leaders exhibit through their decisions and actions.

4. Visible commitment of employees and coworkers to the purpose.

5. Team members see coherence between the purpose and the company's systems and practices.

6. Team members are given the opportunity to reflect and opinionate upon the purpose.

7. Frequent recalling of purpose in all aspects/ activities of the business.

In summary, purpose is the soul of your organization, and in my reflections back on those clients I worked with during the financial crisis, the ones that had a soul and understood their purpose and acted upon it, survived and thrived, those that didn't weren't quite so fortunate. Today this is even more important, and by integrating purpose into all you do, it will breed success and help you create a flourishing organization.

Questions For Thought

1. Do you know your purpose? Write out your organization's purpose in two sentences.

2. Does your team understand your purpose?

3. What is your mission and is your purpose instilled in your mission?

4. How do you support your ongoing purpose? What is your vision and are your guiding beliefs connecting with your mission and vision?

5. Do you have a higher purpose, and is it incorporated into your mission, vision and guiding beliefs?

CHAPTER 2
The Interior Work of Leading Well

Virtue means doing the right thing, in
relation to the right person, at the right
time to the right extent, in the right
manner, for the right purpose.
—Aristotle

I've often wondered in my work with leaders why some of them are energized and excited about their work while other leaders are stressed out and have a hard time dealing with the people they lead. A crisis will really bring these things out. At the onset of COVID, as we had leaders go through the Certificate of Integrated Leadership program that I directed, you could see the differences when they attended the three-day executive retreat. Some were raring to go, while others were just plain tired and stressed. We had to make sure that we gave them all the space and time to understand how important the interior work of leadership is. And to begin the process of first understanding the interior work and why it's important but then to actually do the work that would help them when they left the retreat and went back to reality. This interior work of leadership may be the one most important thing a leader can do to become a better leader.

All leadership begins with the person. The person that leads must exercise living well in order to lead well. Leaders are not born, leaders grow in their capabilities, and if they are not constantly working on themselves, they will lose the ability to lead well. The best leaders I have met over the years and many whom I have worked with have exhibited interior happiness in their lives, and over the years, I've wondered what led them to be that way. Positive psychology is the term credited to the study and science of happiness. This term is most often credited to Dr. Martin Seligman, the founder of the study of positive psychology. Many others have studied this science in both individuals and organizations, and there have been many studies that have shown the benefits of positive psychology to both individuals and organizations.

In my work with clients during the financial crisis, long before I knew anything about positive psychology, I noticed those individuals that were generally happy and passed on that attitude to those who worked within their organizations seemed to be much better at dealing with the crisis. On many occasions, I heard leaders talk about staying positive in light of all the bad news and keeping up optimism throughout those dark days. In those organizations, people were generally much less fearful of the potential consequences of what the crisis might bring. So what was it that gave those leaders the ability to stay positive during those dark days?

The Basis of Positive Psychology: Virtue and Character

Virtue ethics is the contemporary account within philosophy to strengths of character. Virtues pertain to people and the lives they lead. Character strengths emphasize the why and how of good character. Aristotle called leading a virtuous life "leading a life of excellence." In Alexander Havard's book, *The Virtuous Leader*, he states, "What is the context of character? It is virtue, or more precisely, the set of classical human virtues—above all, magnanimity, humility, prudence, courage, self-control and justice." Leading well is directly linked to virtue because virtue creates trust. Simon Sinek, the author of multiple books, including *Start with Why* and *Leaders Eat Last*, talks about the idea that in order to have effective leadership, we must create an environment of safety, and when we have that safety, we then create trust and cooperation which allows for effective, positive leadership.

In his book, *Created for Greatness*, Alexander Havard says that "virtue is a habit acquired through practice. Leadership is a question of character and not of temperament." Dr. Martin Seligman is considered the leading authority on positive psychology; he initially coined the phrase in 1998 in an address to the American Psychological Association. In the study of positive psychology, Dr. Seligman started with virtue and character and their relationship to attaining happiness. In fact, positive psychology is often called the science of happiness. Dr. Seligman's premise was that, up until that time, all psychology had focused on getting people better from the various psychological issues they were having, such as depression, addiction and psychosis. He believed that there should be a study on taking a normal person and making them better and making them happier. And this study isn't some touchy, feely thing where we stand around a circle and sing Kumbaya. It is a scientific approach to achieving happiness.

To start with, he and his team studied many different teachings on virtue and character. In sorting through all these teachings, he and his team identified twenty-four character strengths that were categorized under six virtues: courage, justice, wisdom, temperance, humanity and transcendence. They then went on to create a tool called the Values in Action Inventory, which measured a person's character strengths. This tool measured twenty-four different character traits and categorized them by significance. The top five traits measured were called signature traits and were the top traits that a person exhibited. They were ranked based on the answers to the inventory. Millions of people have used this tool to help them understand the inherent character strengths that they possess.

Seligman also wanted to be clear about what the virtues are versus character. In his book, *Character Strengths and Virtues*, he says, "Virtues are the core characteristics valued by moral philosophers and religious thinkers: wisdom, courage, humanity, justice, temperance and transcendence. These six broad categories of virtue emerge consistently from historical surveys...we argue that these are universal, perhaps grounded in biology through an evolutionary process that selected for these aspects of excellence as means of solving the important tasks necessary for the survival of the species. Character strengths are the psychological ingredients—processes or mechanisms—that define the virtues. Set another way, they are distinguishable routes to displaying one or another of the virtues."

The best leaders I've worked with over the years have embodied these ideas of virtue and character. They understand to lead well, you must act virtuously and display consistent character. In working with leaders using the Values in Action Inventory, one of the primary areas that we focus on is living and working using your character strengths in balance. When I have others rate the leader's top character strengths and match them up with what they found on their assessment, we can begin to talk about what you're doing in balance and what's out of balance. The perception of others is one way to determine if the leader is exercising their character strengths in balance. As I coach leaders through this process, we have to examine what it means to either be using your character strengths too much or too little. In my own assessment using the VIA, I found that one of my character strengths is humor. When I use humor too much, then people don't take me seriously because I'm always joking around. If I use it too little, then they think I'm too serious. So finding that perfect balance is the work of character strengths.

The study of positive psychology is also the study of human flourishing and the traits, habits and behaviors that allow for human flourishing. In the preface of Seligman's book, *Flourishing*, he says, "The content itself happiness, flow, meaning, love, gratitude, accomplishment, growth, better relationships constitutes human flourishing. Learning that you can have more of these things is life-changing."

Positive Leadership: The Heliotropic Effect

Driving down a country road in South Dakota during the summer, it's not unusual to find fields of sunflowers. If you drive down the road in the morning, you will see the sunflowers all pointing toward the east, facing where the sun is coming up. If you go down the same road in the late afternoon, you will see the sunflowers facing west. They have followed the path of the sun. This movement is called the Heliotropic Effect, which says that all living organisms naturally gravitate toward light or toward a positive force. In addition to Dr. Seligman, many others have studied the impacts of happiness, virtue and positivity. Kim Cameron, a professor at the Ross School of Business at the University of Michigan, has studied and written on the Heliotropic Effect and on positive leadership. I have seen the effect of this in organizations that I've worked in, and it is very visible because everyone seems to be happy when you walk in the door.

In his book, *Positive Leadership*, Cameron states, "This book introduces the concept of positive leadership, or the ways in which leaders enable positively deviant performance, foster an affirmative orientation in organizations, and engender a focus on virtuousness and the best of the human condition." Cameron focuses on three aspects of positive leadership. The first is positive deviant performance, or an emphasis on outcomes that exceed common or expected performance. Second, affirmative bias, or a focus on the strengths and capabilities of an individual. And the third is virtuousness, or the facilitation of the best of the human condition. Hundreds of studies have been done on these three aspects, and the research is amazing. Without a doubt, the exercise of virtue, happiness and positivity leads to more healthy, happy and successful people and more productive, profitable and engaged organizations and businesses. Cameron suggests that there are four leadership strategies that can enable positive deviance in an organization. Positive climate, positive meaning, positive relationships and positive communication. Let's examine each of these.

Positive Climate

Positive climate refers to a work environment in which positive emotions dominate over negative emotions. Employees that are optimistic and happy are typical of a positive climate where well-being dominates over distress and dissatisfaction. Leaders are extremely important to a positive climate. Leaders who focus on positive emotions, positive opportunities and positive relationships and stay away from negative threatening and problem issues help to foster a positive climate. That's not to say that they ignore these other issues; however, they deal with them from a positive perspective. Two of the key aspects of a positive climate are forgiveness, an attitude of accepting and moving on from mistakes. The second is gratitude, being grateful for those around you and those opportunities in front of you. The leaders that facilitated these two aspects were able to build much stronger positive cultures.

Positive Relationships

These relationships are not only important from a personal perspective, there is significant research about the psychological, physiological and emotional importance of positive relationships, but Cameron also says this about positive relationships, "Research has revealed that the contributions made to others are what account for the advantages. The demonstration of altruism, compassion, forgiveness, and kindness was found to be necessary for positive relationships to have their maximum positive impact on well-being and performance." The importance of enabling positive relationships in organizations is not news, but the impact of such relationships on multiple factors, including people's emotional and physiological health, life expectancy and positively deviant performance in teams and organizations, is often mentioned; however, giving back to the relationship is as important. Relationships that help people contribute to the benefit of others, rather than merely receive support from them, are the most valuable. Fostering positive energy in the organization and effectively managing positive energizers are also important elements in neighboring these kinds of relationships. Helping individuals and organizations to become aware of and capitalize on their strengths has also been found to predict positive deviant performance, as referenced above.

Positive Communication

Communication in organizations is one of the most important factors that can help determine the success of groups is the method of communication. The ratio of positive statements to negative statements is a key indicator of how well groups perform. Positive statements are those that express appreciation, helpfulness, approval and compliments. The positivity ratio, that being the number of positive communications vs. negative communications, is an important aspect in enabling positive communication in organizations, providing feedback on strengths, unique contributions, and best-self demonstrations support this process.

Positive Meaning

The search for positive meaning has been a basic universal human need. Viktor Frankl, the author of *Man's Search for Meaning*, relates his experience in a Nazi concentration camp and how he found meaning in that horrific experience. He wrote, "that happiness cannot be pursued; it ensues as the result of living a life of meaning and purpose." In recent studies by the Gallup organization, as well as research done by Daniel Pink, meaning and purpose are among the most important aspects of positive work. "When people feel that they are pursuing a profound purpose or engaging in work that is personally important, significant positive effects are produced, including reductions in stress, depression, turnover, absenteeism, dissatisfaction, and cynicism, as well as increases in commitment, effort, engagement, empowerment, happiness, satisfaction, and a sense of fulfillment." (Cameron)

In Jon Gordon's book, *The Power of Positive Leadership*, he sums up the positive leader, "As a result, positive leaders invest their time and energy in driving a positive culture. They create and share the vision for the road ahead. They lead with optimism and belief and address and transform the negativity that too often sabotages teams and organizations. They take on the battle, overcome the negativity, face adversity, and keep moving forward. They devote all their energy and effort to uniting and connecting their organization and invest in relationships to truly build great teams. They believe in their principles. They believe in their people. They believe in their teamwork. They believe in the future. They believe in what's possible. So they act and do, connect and create, build, and transform their team and organization and change the world."

Positive Leadership and Crisis

During the 2008–09 financial crisis, I witnessed in my clients many different reactions and approaches to how organizations dealt with the crisis. Let me give you a couple of examples of how different leaders reacted to the crisis:

Leader 1

This leader immediately hit the panic button. His initial response was to look at his own situation and focus on that and not focus on his company. He worried about his stock portfolio and his personal cash flow and how he was going to maintain his very high standard of living. Not once in the first two weeks of the crisis did he address his team and talk about what they should do, and he constantly worried out loud that his company was going to fail. Of course, this wound up being a self-fulfilling prophecy as they did fail within a year of the onset of the crisis.

Leader 2

Within hours of the Lehman Bros. announcement, this leader gathered his team to discuss the facts as they knew them at that point. He also reassured them that they were going to weather the storm and that no one was going to lose their jobs; the company was in good shape. He also immediately focused on their customers and got his team to understand that at that point in time, it was absolutely crucial that they do all they could to reassure their customers. This organization would survive the crisis and eventually come out of it even stronger than it was before.

These are two very different reactions to the crisis, and they were very different outcomes. Leader 2 was what I call the "positive leader." He believed that they would get through the crisis and also saw a potential opportunity to capitalize on the situation as well by focusing on their customers. We have seen many of these same things during the pandemic, where leaders had to make decisions during uncertain times, and those that made those decisions have survived the pandemic and sometimes even thrived. One of the most impacted industries was restaurants. Having done three restaurant turnarounds, I understand what needs to happen for a restaurant to be successful; however, the pandemic threw out all the normal rules. The behaviors that restaurant owners had to exhibit were crucial to their success. The behaviors that those positive leaders exhibited were crucial to whether they survived and/or thrived through the crisis. Here are five behaviors that many of the ones that survived and thrived exhibited:

1. **Reassure:** Lay out the facts and contain the fallout so that team members can put their own personal fears aside and focus on what needs to be done. In positive psychology, this term is called holding.

2. **Make Decisions Quickly:** Oftentimes, in a crisis, you don't have time to ponder over decisions. They must be made quickly. The key here is to get as much input as possible from team members before being decisive.

3. **Adapt to the Current Situation:** By understanding and adapting to the current situation and realizing that it may mean current goals and objectives won't be met, the leader makes a course correction much like a sailor makes a course correction when the wind changes.

4. **Intense Focus on Stakeholders:** The leader must get their team to focus on customers, suppliers and other stakeholders that impact the future of the organization. The leader also must have an intense focus on the team, always making sure they have time for team members that need more reassurance and help in understanding the situation.

5. **Grab Opportunities:** Some of the most successful leaders I've worked with created opportunities by thinking outside the box and looking for opportunities that maybe weren't there before the crisis. We'll talk more about this in a later chapter.

As we look at the interior work of the leader through the lens of positive psychology, there are certain traits that can help the leader through a crisis situation. These traits are things that can be more fully developed by all leaders and are identified in the Values in Action Inventory. They go to the core of virtue and character—what it means to be a positive leader.

1. **Gratitude:** The ability to be grateful even in less than desirable circumstances.

2. **Realistic Optimism:** Looking at the best possible outcome and practicing looking at the bright side of any situation.

3. **Avoid Overthinking:** In Marshall Goldsmith's book, *What Got You Here, Won't Get You There*, one of the twenty bad habits that he mentions is overthinking things. By avoiding this habit, it allows the leaders to make decisions with speed.

4. **Develop Strategies for Coping:** Creating methods for coping even when the stress is high; this could be spirituality, meditation, coaching or all of the above.

Although I didn't know it at the time, those leaders and organizations that had the tenets of positive psychology in their day-to-day actions were the organizations that survived and thrived during the financial crisis and the pandemic. Positive psychology, or what I like to call the science of virtue, leads to flourishing in people and organizations.

Questions For Thought

1. Do you know your character strengths? If not, go here to take the Values in Action Inventory: https://www.authentichappiness.sas.upenn.edu/testcenter

2. Do you practice exercises that help you grow in happiness? If not, what are some you can do?

3. Do you exercise positive leadership?

4. How can you incorporate positivity in your organization?

CHAPTER 3
Engaging Well: Faith Foundations and Work

Businesses create goods and services and organize the work people do together. Successful businesses design work that is good and effective, efficient and engaging, autonomous and collaborative. The way human work is designed and managed has a significant effect on whether the organization can compete in the marketplace

—Vocation of the Business Leader

Today, businesses and organizations face a crisis within their own walls that they have created and yet can't seem to overcome. In the last fifteen years, Gallup has done surveys of workers in the US, and consistently over that period of time, almost 70 percent of the workers surveyed have said they are either disengaged or actively disengaged in their jobs. That's of the workforce today who does not engage in their work. The drain on productivity is staggering, and yet many organizations either bury their heads in the sand or try and take a band-aid approach to get their people more engaged.

Obviously, something has to change, and as I observed my clients during the financial crisis of 2008–09, I began to notice some things about the ones that were surviving and thriving that were different than the ones who were struggling. That difference was the way their employees were engaged in their work. Over the years, as I have reflected and researched this difference, it became very clear that the engaged organizations practiced what the Catholic Church commonly calls Catholic Social Teaching and what I'll call faith principles. These faith principles always begin with the person, not the work. In my own life, I have clearly seen that when my work is directly connected to my faith and my beliefs, I work better and am more engaged in the work I do, whether it's coaching, consulting or writing. The quality is much better. I try to do a three-day silent retreat occasionally to listen to what God wants of me, and it's during those deeply connected times that I get my best inspiration for my work. I have known clients that do some form of this listening and have similar results. So connecting faith principles to work is not only good for the soul, but it's good for the work. Let's examine some of those faith principles that led my clients and their teams to be more engaged, productive and loyal.

First Principle: Dignity of the Human Person

In the Christian tradition, we believe that man is created in the image and likeness of God. This is brought out in Genesis 1:26–27. Human dignity is understood as flowing from one's relationship with God and is not earned or merited. The principle of human dignity rests on a foundation of faith, which affirms that God is the source and creator of all life. In the document *The Vocation of the Business Leader*, human dignity is addressed, "Because of human dignity, each person has the right-indeed the obligation-to pursue his or her vocation and to strive for personal fulfillment in community with others. In turn, this also entails that each of us has a duty to avoid actions that impede the flourishing of others and, as far as possible, a duty to promote that flourishing, for we are all really responsible for all." I strongly believe that if we had more people exercising this whole idea of human dignity, many of the problems and controversial ideas of the day would go away. The whole movement of DEI (diversity, equality and inclusion) would not even exist if we all treated each other with dignity and respect. We wouldn't have the divisions, rage and hate that we have today if the idea of dignity were exercised. Dignity is a very powerful principle that we do a very poor job of executing.

Second Principle: The Vocation of Work

Meaning and purpose in one's work are vital to the success of that work. In his book *Drive*, Daniel Pink discusses the whole idea of purpose at work. In the earlier chapter on purpose, I talked about organizational purpose, but the other aspect of purpose is individual purpose. Pope John Paul II wrote about the nature of work in his encyclical called *Laborum Execens*. In that document, he says, "Through work, man must earn his daily bread and contribute to the continual advance of science and technology, and above all, to elevating unceasingly the cultural and moral level of the society within which he lives in community with those who belong to the same family. And work means any activity by man, whether manual or intellectual, whatever its nature or circumstances; it means any human activity that can and must be recognized as work, by virtue of humanity itself... Work is one of the characteristics that distinguish man from the rest of creatures, whose activity for sustaining their lives cannot be called work. Only man is capable of work, and only man works, at the same time by occupying his existence on earth. Thus, work bears a particular mark of man on humanity; the mark of a person operating within a community of persons. And this mark decides its interior characteristics; in a sense, it constitutes its very natures."

Today meaning and purpose at work have become more important than the paycheck received. Working where one feels there is more to the work than the work itself, but also a greater purpose and opportunity that the work itself contributes to a greater good is a driving factor in engagement. Victor Frankl, the author of *Man's Search for Meaning,* talks about his experiences in a Nazi concentration camp and how a person can survive anything if they find the meaning and purpose, finding meaning in life even in the horrific circumstances of this adversity finding meaning in life becomes essential.

In Dave and Wendy Ulrich's book *The Why of Work,* they talk about the meaning of work, "That's the search for meaning and value in two senses of the word. First, humans are meaning-making machines who find inherent value in making sense out of life. The meaning we make of an experience determines its impact on us and can turn disaster into opportunity, lost into hope, failure into learning, boredom into reflection. The meaning we create can make life feel rich and full regardless of our external circumstances or give us the courage to change our external circumstances. When we find meaning in our work, we find meaning in life. In addition to inherent value, meaning has market value. Meaningful work solves real problems, contributes real benefits, and adds real value to customers and investors. Employees who find meaning in their work are more satisfied, more engaged, and in turn, more productive. They work harder, smarter, more passionately and creatively. They learn and adapt. They are more connected to customer needs. And they stick around. Leaders invest in meaning-making not only because it is noble but also because it is profitable."

Businesses and organizations create work to move that entity forward in the creation of goods and services. As organizations of work were created over the centuries, many of them looked at the individual as just a cog in the wheel, and unfortunately, many organizations still look at their people that way today, nothing more than a means to an end to produce profit for their shareholders. It is one of the main reasons I believe that engagement numbers are so low across all organizations. Creating good and productive work puts the person at the forefront, not just an end to a means, and many organizations are now looking at this as a very important piece of what they do. The whole idea or principle of creating good and productive work focuses on the idea that human work not only leads to improved products and services but also develops the worker themselves and gives them what Pope John Paul II taught, "when people work, they don't just make more, they become more." As we are coming out of a global pandemic, businesses and organizations will have an entirely different idea of work and the value of making sure people are doing good and productive work, whether it's in person or remotely. This new dynamic will offer opportunities for leaders to directly engage their teams in new and different ways of doing the work that needs to be done.

Third Principle: The Common Good and Business

In the previous chapter, I talked about higher purpose, which can also be stated as a pursuit of the common good. Contributing positively to those around us, our environment and our community enhances our work and gives us the sense that our work is for more than just financial gain. The idea of the common good has been around for a long time, but it is gaining more and more traction in the business world. As I mentioned in the chapter on purpose, many organizations now are focusing on stakeholder value versus shareholder value. How does this impact engagement? As humans, we have a desire to do something with meaning and purpose, but also that impacts something greater than ourselves. When we talk about the common good, we are talking about doing for others. In Tom Nelson's book *Work Matters*, he says, "When we speak of the common good, we are describing all the various aspects of contemporary life that contribute positively to human flourishing both as individuals and as communities. The Protestant reformers connected location to human flourishing and the common good. Martin Luther's understanding of vocation was deeply embedded in our calling as workers promote the well-being of others and our world. Anchoring his thoughts in Jesus's great commandment to love our neighbor as ourselves, Martin Luther made the seminal point that while God doesn't really need our good works, our neighbor clearly does. Luther's theology of vocation emphasizes the primary way we love our neighbor as in and through our work. John Calvin also saw human work through the lens of the common good. Calvin said, "it is not enough when one can say, oh I work, I have my trade, I set the pace." this is not enough; for one must be concerned whether it is good and profitable to the community and if it is able to serve our neighbors."

A good business is a business that creates goods and services for its customers in a way that also looks toward the common good. The book *The Good Business Does* by Robert G. Kennedy is all about good business. In his book, he says, "A good business must also attend to the constructive common goods that shape and organization. These goods have to do with the conditions under which the organization conducts its activities and are analogous to the common good of a Civic Community. A good business is one in which these conditions are established and sustained. In general, they would include the rudiments of good management, such as clear communication, consistent and reasonable policies; safe working conditions; and a widely accepted culture in which fairness, honesty, and respect for persons are valued and respected. Management, of course, has a primary responsibility for creating and sustaining such a culture, but this responsibility is shared with every member of the organization. Because this is a common good, all members of the organization have a duty to sustain its sound aspects by their behavior and a duty to avoid behaviors that would have the effect of undermining it. In sum, a good business is a good place to work."

Fourth Principle: Engaging Well— Subsidiarity and Empowerment

Two other principles that must be considered in raising engagement are the principles of subsidiarity and solidarity. Let's examine each. Subsidiarity is defined in an organizational sense as a moral principle that directs leaders to place decision-making at the most appropriate level of an organization. In the book *Respect in Action* by Naughton, Buckeye, Goodpaster and Maines, say this about subsidiarity, "Subsidiarity... places decision-making at the most appropriate level of an organization so as to utilize the gifts of employees for their own good, the good of the organization, and the good of the organization's clients or customers. In practice, it serves several important ends: it helps employees develop through their work, it builds trust among the leaders and subordinates, and it strengthens the identity and culture of a firm. Subsidiarity is based on the understanding that each person has a right to be respected and that each person

Bears gifts to be exercised. Leaders are at their best, according to this principle, when they build organizations that actively drop on the diverse gifts (talents, abilities, and skills) of all employees."

The principle of subsidiarity requires certain things to be successful, from the Vocation of the Business Leader, "specifically, this principle engages business leaders in three related responsibilities:

1. To define the scope of autonomy and decision-making at every level in the company. The business leader should allow these to be as significant as possible, but set clear limits, so that decision rights do not exceed a person or groups access to the information required to make the decision, and so that their decisions do not have consequences beyond their realm of responsibility.

2. To provide employees the needed tools and training to ensure that they have the knowledge and skills to carry out their tasks.

3. To establish a corporate culture of trust so that those to whom tasks and responsibilities have been given will make their decisions with genuine freedom. The company, informed by subsidiarity, nurtures mutual respect and shared responsibility among all persons. It allows employees to clearly appreciate the link between good results and their sincere engagement.

This last point about decision-making is what distinguishes subsidiarity from delegation. Someone who delegates confers responsibility or decision-making power, but it can be taken back at any time. So, delegation does not call employees to the same level of excellence, and genuine engagement as do arrangements governed by the principle of subsidiarity, and thus, the employees are less likely to grow into accepted full responsibility."

Subsidiarity is a principle that not only encourages but requires engagement in order to succeed and to create human and organizational flourishing.

Empowerment is a buzzword we often hear today in corporate circles; however, empowerment is different from subsidiarity in that empowerment is conceived to mean to obtain better results or competitive advantages. Empowerment has been considered in the context of strategies and tactics as resource allocation to increase the power of the less powerful parties and reduce the power of the more powerful ones. The purpose of subsidiarity is to create structures in which persons can flourish as humans.

Rules of Engagement

So now that we have examined some of the faith principles that can improve engagement, let's put them to work. Here are seven rules that can build engagement in any organization.

Challenging Work

Design work that challenges employees and allows them to exercise their talents and gifts to the best of their ability. Also, in work design, creating an environment where people can move up as their skills and talents increase motivates them to continue to grow as human beings.

Company Reputation

Maintaining and protecting the company's reputation is essential to good engagement. People want to work for a company that is respected in its endeavors and does what it says it will do. We only need to look at cases such as Enron, where they said one thing and then did a totally different thing and what that did to their reputation, let alone their entire business.

Company's Care and Concern for Employees

By providing for employees through programs that exhibit company concern and care, employees get a sense that they are not just a cog in the wheel but that someone actually cares about them as a person. Employee benefit programs, support programs and opportunities for employees to support one another build a community, not just an organization.

Evidence that the company is customer-focused

Laser-focused on customers versus products. A company that doesn't take care of its customers is most likely short-lived, but it always amazes me how many companies focus on either the owners' take or the shareholders' profit at the expense of customers. During the financial crisis, I saw several companies so concerned that the owner was going to be alright that they neglected the customer, and, in the end, that was their undoing.

Resources to Get the Job Done

In order for employees to be engaged, they must be able to do their jobs well. Organizations that focus on training and development of their teams will have a much higher engagement level. Also, providing resources to do the job right, such as supplies, materials, processes and systems, will create an environment where employees can feel like the organization backs them up in their job responsibilities.

Clear Purpose and Vision

We spent an entire chapter on purpose and vision, but from an employee engagement perspective, it means that the purpose and vision are clearly communicated and are infused into all aspects of the organization.

Appreciation

Reward does not just mean fair pay for fair work but also the appreciation and celebration of personal and organizational achievements and goals attained. Appreciation should be genuine and sincere and should be made as a very big deal.

Engagement is one of the key elements for success in any organization today; however, during a crisis, it becomes even more essential. If employees are disengaged during a crisis, there are all kinds of bad things that can happen, from losing customers due to poor customer service to creating below average goods and services, to loss of productivity and the expense of it and detrimental press and PR that can give an organization a bad reputation. All these things increase tenfold during a crisis, and exercising the rules of engagement to build a foundation for excellent employee engagement will pay huge dividends during normal times but especially in a crisis. There are many tools to help determine employee engagement, including the Gallup Organization's Q12 tool. Another tool that I like to use is the tool developed by The University of Pennsylvania called the PERMA At Work tool. This inventory developed by Martin Seligman and his team measures how engaged employees are at work by looking at positive emotion, engagement, relationships, meaning and achievement. By understanding these aspects of employee engagement and how positive psychology and faith principles can deeply affect engagement, we develop flourishing teams and employees.

Questions For Thought

1. How engaged is your team? One good way to find out is to have people do the PERMA exercise here: https://www.authentichappiness.sas. upenn. edu/testcenter

2. Do you allow decision-making at the lowest level that it can be made?

3. Do you show appreciation for your team?

4. Do you spend time with team members getting to know them and encouraging them?

CHAPTER 4
A Fifteen-Hundred-Year-Old
Guide to Leading Well

It is not so among you, but whoever
wishes to become great among you
shall be your servant, and whoever
wishes to be first among you shall be
your slave; just as the Son of Man did
not come to be served, but to serve and
to give His life a ransom for many.

—Matthew 20:25–28

Many leadership programs today are called deficit-based leadership programs. Meaning they are programs designed to help leaders find issues and problems that can make them better or make their organizations better. These programs address how leaders make things better by focusing on negative issues. I believe there is a better way to approach leadership based on timeless teachings that focus on the strengths of people and organizations and encourage the development of positive leaders. Ideas that talk about the development of the person and how they live and work in the community and how they can flourish. So how can a document written fifteen hundred years ago during the collapse of Rome possibly be a blueprint for leading well today? The Rule of St. Benedict lays out a foundation for personal development while living and working within the community and, by doing so, gives us a wonderful roadmap. I was introduced to this time-tested document over four years ago, and the more I study it, the more I believe that it is one of the greatest organizational blueprints ever created. I've seen a large health care company still operate using the blueprint and doing it very effectively. Companies and institutions around the world use this "Rule" as their user's manual on how they exist and are successful.

What is the Rule? History

Today's business seems a far cry from a sixth-century monastery. Nevertheless, the principles of Benedict's life and work speak well to today's world. Benedict of Nursia was born around the year 480 into a noble family. As a young man, he was sent to Rome to study. However, he quickly witnessed the collapse of the Roman Empire, and so he fled south to the hills of Subiaco to follow the hermit's life. He soon realized that the answer to his own problems and the problems of the world was to be found not in solitary escape but in laying the foundations of a society based on prayer.

The Roman Empire had crumbled by Benedict's time, and in the midst of collapsing institutions, moral decay and social chaos, Benedict established religious communities based on work, prayer and routine. Drawing on earlier monastic writings, Benedict created a very simple document, a rule that lays down the principles of monastic life. The Rule of St. Benedict is a classic of Christian spirituality and the fact that it's still followed by monks and nuns fifteen hundred years after its composition shows its continued relevance. The Rule is not so much a spiritual treatise as a practical guide for living and working with others. It gives detailed instructions on the monks' liturgical life, but it also provides down-to-earth guidelines for the proper qualities of an abbot, prior and cellarer (the leaders of the community). It outlines how the monks must constantly listen, respect and forgive one another and the attitude they should have toward material things. In a famous line, Benedict noted that the vessels of the kitchen must be treated with the same reverence as the vessels of the altar. Throughout his rule, St. Benedict emphasized the importance of routine as work, prayer and community life. For Benedict, the spiritual life was not a great ascetic ascent to holiness. Instead, holiness is found in the routine, the mundane and the ordinary.

Why is it Important Today?

I've had the opportunity to study The Rule over the past two years, teaching it to undergrad students and for my own reflection on becoming a Benedictine oblate. The Rule is a very simple document with seventy-three short chapters organized around what is called *Ora et Labora* prayer and work. The document examines how a community of monks can live and work within the community. It is today's version of organizational excellence—a set of procedures and systems that allow the community to excel—sort of an ISO9000 from the sixth century. Unlike many other historical documents, what is unique about the Rule is that it is an actual written document that has not changed over fifteen hundred years. It is not some interpretation of something that was said or written; it's the actual real deal. In Quentin Skrabec's *St. Benedict's Rule for Business Success,* he says, "Benedict's rule is both an organizational Constitution and a philosophy. In this respect, Benedict addresses organizational infrastructure as well as the heart and soul of organizations." He goes on to say, "The rule promoted learning and information systems. Benedictine monasteries were true examples of what today we call learning organizations. These monasteries became knowledge-based organizations that excelled in innovation and invention." The Rule gives us a clear blueprint of organizational excellence. In addition, it addresses the leader (abbot) and how they should lead the organization.

In the book *The Benedictine Rule of Leadership*, Craig and Oliver Galbraith state, "The rule deals almost exclusively with the internal workings of organizations. It focuses on proper management, motivation, and organization of daily work, and the most basic, but often forgotten, Universal principles of leadership. Benedict concentrated on the core bedrock principles that motivated people of all cultures. He believed that the individual leader, under the guidance of these unbreakable basic rules of leadership, would be able to successfully adapt to the individual situation as necessary regardless of time or place."

Benedict wrote the Rule with two distinct objectives, that of the organization and that of the leader. Benedict believed in keeping it short and sweet, and his words were meant not to be "harsh or burdensome." The Rule was not only meant for monastic life in the sixth century, but Benedict understood that it must face the test of time. In the fifteen hundred years since the Rule was written, its leadership and organizational principles have been used in hospitals, universities, corporations and monastic communities that have excelled for hundreds of years. Unlike the latest fad in organizational leadership, the Rule was meant for longevity. Galbraiths go on to say, "Why is organizational longitude important to the study of management and leadership? Because longevity is a very rare commodity in the history of organizations. Longevity is an indication of a sustainable organization or system. It is an indication of something that honestly merits intense study and deep understanding. In the literature of modern leadership theory, most of what we profess to study are really infant organizations struggling with their first baby steps on the world stage. We generally ignore the real lessons of history."

Interior Principles of the Leader

The Rule focuses on the interior work of the leader and principles that he thought were most important to the leaders and the community's excellence. The first of those interior principles is listening. The Rule starts by saying, "listen carefully, my son, to the master's instructions, and attend to them with the ear of your heart." Benedict believed that for the leader to lead well, then they must practice active listening. If you study the Chinese character for intense listening, it has four parts: ears, eyes, undivided attention and heart. This is what Benedict had in mind when he started the Rule. In Michael Rock's book, *St. Benedict's Guide to Improving Your Work Life,* he says, "Listening involves and attends to, a giving over to oneself, a giving beyond oneself. It is truly an eccentric activity—the ability to stand outside our own self, our own personal concerns, as legitimate as they may be, and truly see the other. In this attending to the other, two movements take place: 1) understanding the other person and 2) showing empathy with the other person. Both dimensions are required. In other words, can I understand this person in what is being said or done, and can I appreciate this person just for being who they are? Can I listen by attending to these two movements and noticing what is happening?" By "listening with the ear of your heart," the leader steps outside themselves to be open to what the person is saying and then best deciding how to respond.

Authority and Decision Making

In the Rule, the abbot is where the buck stops. However, the process that the abbot takes to get to this final decision is not an authoritarian process. It is rooted in a democratic process that allows constant feedback and input. Although authority is granted to the abbot in the Rule, the abbot takes into account the feedback from other members of the community. In addition, the abbot allows the decision-making process to start from the bottom up. As we examined in a previous chapter, in the concept of subsidiarity, the Rule addresses this process. Benedict's idea of authority also is tied to obedience and a chain of command that focuses on first upper-level leaders and then the more experienced individuals of the community. Experience counts in Benedict's process of leadership. In addition, the leader assumes authority through teaching, and it's the leader's responsibility to teach and lead by example through servant leadership.

In the book *The Art of Leadership* by Notker Wolf and Enrica Rosanna, they write, "Benedict considered authority only justifiable and good when official power was paired with concern for the individual, when it was combined with respect for individuality, different abilities, and particular personal needs. When Benedict extolls the Abbot with far-reaching powers, this is not only because someone has to have the final say but because he understands Authority as an instance that helps, supports, encourages, and exhorts, and is constantly mindful of the progress and welfare of those who are subject to it. The purpose of real authority is there for all ways to help people to become more independent and discover what lies within their capabilities: in other words, help them to become free."

Humility

One of the most important aspects of the Rule is humility; in fact, Benedict spends more time on this in the Rule than any other aspect. Chapter 7 of the Rule ends with these words, "Having climbed all these steps of humility, therefore, the monk will presently come to that perfect love of God which casts out fear. And all those precepts which formerly he had not observed without fear, he will now begin to keep by reason of that love, without any effort, as though naturally and by habit. No longer will his motive be the fear of hell, but rather the love of Christ, good habit and delight in the virtues with the Lord will deign to show forth by the Holy Spirit in his servant now cleansed from vice and sin."

In Andre Havard's book, *Created for Greatness*, he defines humility as "The habit of serving others. Humility means pulling rather than pushing, teaching rather than ordering about, inspiring rather than berating. Plus, leadership is less about displays of power than the empowerment of others. To practice humility is to bring out the greatness in others, to give them the capacity to realize their human potential." Benedict believed the virtue of humility was particularly important in leadership positions because it meant the leader must exercise discretion, compassion, and moderation in command.

Benedict lays out his Steps of Humility in Chapter 7 of the Rule. From Galbraith's book, *The Benedictine Rule of Leadership*, here is a modern version of the steps.

"In the rule, Benedict defines 12 Progressive steps on the ladder to learning true humility. In modern terms, they are:

Step 1: Revere The Simple Rules. Start by following Simple Rules calling don't speed, stop at red lights, meet deadlines.

Step 2: Reject your personal desires. Consciously tamper your basic desires, fast when a little hungry, avoid impulse buying, skip dessert after dinner.

Step 3: Obey others. Willingly and without any internal grumbling, obey others in positions of authority.

Step 4: Endure affliction. Consciously turn the other cheek when upset, even if you are in the right.

Step 5: Confess your weaknesses. Regularly acknowledge, even to just yourself, your failings. Spell out the details.

Step 6: Practice contentment. Try to be content with your job, status in life, and the old car.

Step 7: Learn self-reproach. Develop a conscious effort to see yourself as humble and truly lucky to have whatever you have in life. This requires serious internal reflection.

Step 8: Obey the common rule. Obey all the organizational rules, not just in letter, but also in spirit. In particular, follow the Rule of Benedict.

Step 9: Understand that silence is golden. Consciously try to listen more than speak. Don't give as many executive orders.

Step 10: Meditate on humility. Meditate on the seriousness of humility, and let this seriousness enter into your actions and speech.

Step 11: Speak simply. Talk in a low voice, speak gently, and with kindness to everyone.

Step 12: Be humble in appearance. Be humble in appearance as well as in art. Tone down the expensive dress and elegant taste.

Benedict reminds us to study these steps but, above all, to practice them and live them in everyday life. The rule recognizes that executive humility is a complex emotion. True humility is learned by attempting the first step reverence to simple ideas then moving progressively higher with practice."

Benedictine Keys to Effective Organizations

Benedict's Rule is a blueprint for organizational effectiveness but also a philosophy. In Skrabec's book, *St. Benedict's Rule for Business Success*, says, "Benedict addresses organizational infrastructure as well as the heart and soul of organizations. Benedict realized that laws and rules, while necessary and foundational, could not save Rome. That philosophy of quality and Benedict's view that Faith must have priority over rules were the basis on which the rule was conceived. The power of Benedict's Rule today is its ability to integrate rules and philosophy. This integration brings an understanding to rules and laws that allows obedience and loyalty."

The Rule touches on four areas of the organization, stability, excellence, hospitality and teamwork. These four areas represent the core of the community.

Stability: In Benedict's time, it was not uncommon for monks to wander from monastery to monastery looking for the grass to be greener, and he believed this practice to be detrimental to the community. He also understood that stability meant continuity, and because of that, the Rule stated that once a monk was accepted into the community, they could not leave.

There were three keys to stability: community, fairness and tenure. Benedict was very family-oriented, and he believed that the structure of the monastery was similar to the structure of a family. Bob Chapman, the CEO of Barry Wehmiller, references this idea of the organization as a family in a great YouTube video called the "Crisis of Leadership." The organization must also be committed to fairness, which Benedict referred to as an even-handedness, is dealing with the members of the community. And lastly, Benedict believed that tenure was the key to longevity, and therefore members must commit to a lifetime in the community, that however, would be rewarded by being part of the family and its benefits.

Hospitality

One of the more interesting parts of the Rule was the way meals were to be done, and especially the way guests were to be accepted. This tradition is still an important part of monasteries throughout the world today. The "breaking of bread" was a very important part of community life, and when the community welcomed guests into their meals, they received an exalted position.

I remember working with a client several years ago, and as I met with the employees, they told me that one of the more important things the owner did was to throw a barbeque every Friday afternoon, and they would get to openly discuss what was going on with the company and they would also welcome guests like customers and vendors. I can say that over thirty years of doing business, I have probably done more business over a meal than sitting at someone's desk. I think Benedict was onto something here. Hospitality is the idea of welcoming, and that was an important part of the Benedictine community.

Excellence

Benedictine monasteries are known throughout the world for some of their products. Whether it's brewing beer, making liquors, aging wine, growing mushrooms or other products, the quality of those products is renowned. The foundation to the quality comes from the Rule, and the commitment to excellence in all the monks do. In August Turks' book, *Business Secrets of the Trappist Monks,* he says, "The abbeys fanatical commitment to quality is just the byproduct of living life with a prayerful attitude. Excellence for the sake of excellence is what really motivates the monks and drives their monastic businesses. The secret to the monk success is not that they have managed to establish the mythical healthy balance between their personal and professional lives the secret is that their personal, organizational, and business lives are all subsets of their one, high, overarching mission becoming the best human beings they can possibly be."

Teamwork

For the monastery to be a cohesive organization, it was imperative that all community members could rely on each other. This term is called "mutual reliance", and it is the basis for teamwork in the community. The first aspect of this is mutual respect, by doing things together and functioning as a team, members must all respect each other no matter what their job or role is.

To build a cohesive team, Benedict realized that there would be layers of jobs and importance; however, he warned against it. In the *Benedictine Rule of Leadership*, Galbraith wrote, "Benedict acknowledged that certain activities of design and production have a more direct link to the corporate bottom line than others in high technology sectors. A company's future hinges on the innovative abilities of its engineers and scientists. And university professors are the ones who teach, research, publish, and raise grant money. Benedict recognized this fundamental fact but also carefully warned that a cohesive organization must think and work as a unit. To Benedict, it was an issue of attitude, not role or position. As soon as one group of individuals sets itself apart, demanding a higher level of treatment, then by definition, the organization has a discriminatory class system and is no longer 'cohesive.'" We can see this impact in many organizations today, and I experienced it first-hand in many of the banks I worked with. They called it the silo effect, and each unit of the organization was protecting its turf, and no one was allowed to interfere. The interesting aspect of this is that once the walls came down and the silos were broken up, people began to create new ideas and ways of doing things that they would never have come up with in protecting their silos.

The fifteen-hundred-year-old Rule of Benedict gives us a framework today for leadership and flourishing organizations. Benedict understood the crisis as he wrote the Rule during one of the biggest crises in the history of the world. However, he also understood that the crisis was short-term and that organizations must be built for longevity. The Rule gives leaders and organizations today key principles that they can lead with and create positive, flourishing organizations.

Questions For Thought

1. Are you a humble leader? Are you practicing the steps to humility?

2. How do you treat your employees like a family?

3. Do you allow for individuality within your organization structure, and if so, how does it allow for individuals to contribute to the community?

4. Are you committed to excellence in all you do? What quality standards do you set and does everyone follow them?

CHAPTER 5
Strategy During a Crisis: The Key to Survival and Recovery

When written in Chinese, the word crisis
is composed of two characters. One
represents danger, the other opportunity.

—John F. Kennedy

In 2011, I wrote a whitepaper called *9 Core Principles to Maximize Profits*. This article was in direct response to inquiries from clients on ways that they could become profitable again in light of the financial crisis. In the paper, I laid out nine principles with three strategies under each of those principles. As I look back on that document, many of those strategies are still important today. Some of them are fundamentals, the blocking and tackling of business success. They are both familiar and practiced by many organizations. Others may not be familiar or tried, but in my experience, they work very well. The key to all of these strategies is execution; you must take action and implement them for them to work. Two management gurus that have been especially influential in my work over the years are Tom Peters and Jay Abraham. Peters for his sound business sense and Abraham for his cutting-edge marketing strategies. These strategies are the fruit of extensive research and real-world testing with clients in over fifty different industries.

Authority

People want to do business with someone they believe is the authority in what they are looking for. Being known as an authority gives you an immediate leg up against your competitors. So how do you become an authority? The best way is to engage in what I call educational marketing. This type of marketing has nothing to do with your product or service but is strictly designed to provide your potential customers with education regarding what they are looking for from your product or service. By educating them and helping them make better-educated decisions, you position yourself as an authority and the "go-to" person on the topic.

How do you do education marketing? There are many ways. It could be a special report or white paper (you're reading a form of education marketing), it could be an e-course, it could be a blog, and it could be articles you post on Facebook or LinkedIn. There are many ways to create education marketing; the most important thing is to sit down and do it. I often have clients tell me, "I'm not a good writer." Then write your thoughts and have someone else proofread it so that the form is good.

You will find that the sooner you position yourself and your business as an authority, the sooner people will be seeking you out to do business. Another way to do this is by providing information to groups. This could be done in seminars, workshops or through guest speakers. I used this method extensively when working with banks and financial advisors to help them understand the concepts of doing business the way I was proposing to them.

Speed to Market

Speed to market means just that, how quickly can you get something out to your customers and prospective customers. How quickly you get information out to customers and a prospective customer is critical, as well as how quickly you respond to people talking about your business, product, or service. Twitter is a great tool for having conversations with people talking about your business and building a community that supports your business. The key to Twitter working is that you monitor it, so you know when people are talking about you, and you put out things on Twitter that get people talking about you. Social media is an essential tool for the strategy of speed to market because you can quickly get information out, and if you have done a good job of building your community, you can start conversations with potential customers. Plus, if your content is good, it could go viral and get you even better positioned for people to find you and engage in your business. One important point about social media, however, is that it can also be a weapon, meaning that someone can say something about you that may very well be far from the truth and cause considerable damage. All we have to do is look at some of the things happening in politics and in society today and understand that social media can be good and it can be very bad. The moral of the story is to closely monitor your social media so you can not only get information out quickly but that you can react quickly to bad information that's put out against you.

The other important thing to remember about speed to market is that whenever someone starts talking about you and your business, you want to engage in the conversation immediately in order to capitalize on the conversation. There are many tools available to monitor what people are saying about your business, products and services that you can use to monitor without it taking hours of your time. Social media and its various platforms such as Twitter, Facebook, Instagram, Pinterest and Snapchat offer organizations many different opportunities to get information to market. However, that must also be tempered with the fact that they can also get bad news to market quickly too. Making sure you have social media policies in place so that people know what can and can't be shared is critical.

Direct Response

One of the biggest mistakes that many businesses make is to create marketing or advertising for their product or service and spend a lot of money doing it and then, after the fact, realizing there was no call to action in the ad or marketing piece, so there was nothing that would get people to do something to engage with you.

Direct response marketing is the most effective form of marketing you can do, period! Every single marketing tactic should have some form of direct response in it. It gives customers and potential customers the immediate opportunity to engage with you and respond to what you're showing them. It also allows you to measure every aspect of your marketing, which is extremely important. You will know the effectiveness of each of your campaigns simply by measuring the response. It also allows you to test multiple messages to find out which are the most effective.

The key to direct response marketing is that you want to make an offer of some sort that the potential customer or customer can respond to. It may be bringing in a coupon, going online to do a survey, downloading an article, e-book or white paper. It may be something as simple as signing up for a newsletter. But by engaging the person you are targeting, you are bringing them into your marketing funnel. I've had many clients over the years ask me to review their websites, and one of the first things I look for is the opportunity to engage with them. Can I request more information, can I download something, can I have a live chat engagement. These are all methods of direct response, and it never ceases to amaze me how many websites and how many supposed professional website designers completely miss this step in marketing and getting customers and potential customers to engage.

Multiple Channels

When I talk about multiple channels, what I'm talking about is finding different ways and places to sell your product or service. If you are a retail business, is there a way you can sell online? If you are working with a specific industry, is there another industry that could benefit from your product or service? Could your product or service be tweaked a little to open up another market?

Selling in multiple channels allows you to think about new ways to offer your product or service. It allows you to think outside the box and come up with new ways to generate revenue. I saw a story recently about a construction company that had heavy equipment, and because of the slow construction industry, they had equipment sitting idle. They thought completely outside the box and decided to create an amusement theme park for adults by letting them drive and work the heavy equipment. Similar to an amusement park, you could come in and purchase time driving and operating the equipment. It was a huge success and has become a major stream of revenue, and it was totally thinking about multiple channels that got them to make that move.

Have a brainstorming session with your team and think about ways and places that you are not currently selling and marketing that would be an additional revenue stream. You never know. You may find a channel that is even more profitable than your primary business. One of the best examples of multiple channels has come out of the pandemic with restaurants. The ones that didn't close during the pandemic had to quickly figure out a way to still provide food to customers, and they did that by quickly converting their operations to take out or delivery. Most of those restaurants had never done that before, but if they were going to survive, they had to do it. And what's most interesting is that they have now opened up to in-house dining again and are still offering take-out and delivery. That's doing business with multiple channels.

Leverage Customer Assets

One of the most critical core principles for any business is to understand that their customers are one of their most important assets, and how they care for and leverage that asset is essential to both surviving a crisis and creating success. In my book *Ultimate Breakthrough Planning*, I state that there are only three ways to grow a business. More customers, more sales from existing customers, and larger sales from existing customers. And it's far easier to get more sales from existing customers than it is to get new customers. But to do that, you need to first understand that your customer base is your greatest asset and tapping into that asset can lead to dramatic increases in profitability.

I remember meeting with a client a few years ago that had a well-developed business and was trying to figure out how to grow the business by 20 percent. His sales team was strictly focused on getting new customers, and 90 percent of their time was spent doing that. He was not advertising or keeping up with existing customers. When I analyzed what they were doing and realized that they had a customer base of over five thousand customers that had never been marketed, there was a gold mine sitting right inside their database. We shifted the sales team's focus to existing customers and started marketing ancillary products to those customers. In the first year, they grew the business by over 50 percent. Understanding the value of a customer as an asset is crucial. And taking good care of existing customers fits within all the other ideas we have talked about in this book.

Customer Analysis

Analyze your current customers—what are they buying, how often are they buying, what are their buying patterns? How often are you connecting with them or touching them? Most businesses can't answer those questions. They simply react to their customers buying, and they don't clearly understand the relationship they have with that customer. The only way to get customers to buy more or create larger sales is to understand that customer as thoroughly as possible.

Create a list of your best customers and determine what they bought from you and how often they bought from you. Make sure you're collecting information from them so that you can actively touch them through different marketing efforts. The more often you reach out to them, the more of an opportunity you have to increase sales.

Having a strong customer database is the first step in leveraging customer assets and building additional profits from your existing customers. Many CRM (customer relationship management) tools are available today for customer analysis and are a very simple and low-cost way to understand your customers. Some of these tools are free or cost just a few dollars a month, and they are worth the investment to monitor what your customers are doing.

Customer Opportunities

The next step after you have built your database is identifying buying opportunities from your existing customers. Some questions to ask here would be, how do we enhance the buying experience to get them to buy more? What other products can we sell them based on their buying habits? How can we increase the frequency of them buying from us?

The best thing to do is to start creating a priority list of customers that you want to reach out to with ideas that can get them to do more business with you. Then start implementing marketing that focuses on that specific buying opportunity. Also, look at how you currently upsell and cross-sell your customers. Are you doing a good job of getting additional sales based on the processes you're using to do that?

Have a very specific plan on how to identify customer opportunities and then how to implement a sales and marketing plan to add additional sales to those customers. Also, make sure that customers understand the true benefits of the products or services you offer so they can determine when to do business with you.

Exceptional Service vs Customer Experience

It goes without saying that without good customer service, you probably won't be in business very long. However, very few businesses I've encountered really look at customer service as a way to grow profitability. By delivering what I call exceptional service or, as Tom Peters calls it, a "wow experience," you can create profits and not just goodwill. Here are three strategies that focus on delivering exceptional service.

Customer Experience

What customer experiences do you deliver to your customers, especially your best customers? What experience makes a customer say, "wow"? When I ask this question in my seminars, I more often than not get bad customer experiences rather than good ones, but when the good ones come out, they are typically great. The most important point to remember about great customer service is that it doesn't cost a thing. It is the one strategy that can significantly impact the bottom line, yet most businesses do very little to focus on it.

The first step in delivering great customer experience is to define what that means to your business. What is it that you want your customers to say or do when they do business with you? Once you have determined that, then determine how you deliver that and what you will need to do with your team to train them on delivering that level of service. The other idea that I recommend to my clients is to also determine who your top customers are and is there something else you can do at an even higher level for your best customers. Again, this doesn't have to cost a lot, but the value of having your best customers spread the word is invaluable. With this strategy, you want to create raving fans, and if you and your team haven't read Ken Blanchard's book *Raving Fans*, I highly recommend it. One of the great stories I tell in my seminars is about a customer service person that I used to know at Nordstrom at the Mall of America. I would go into the store there maybe twice a year and look for a particular brand of men's clothing I liked. I saw the same woman working in the department a few times. She would immediately recognize me and not only know what brand I was looking for but also my size and would take me over to the sale rack first. If you think about the number of people that went through that department at the Mall of America a year and the fact that I might be in there one or two times a year, it was always amazing to me that she knew exactly what I was looking for. That's what I call a customer experience.

Negative to Positive

The next strategy under this core principle is what I call negative to positive. The best way to explain this is through two recent experiences I had in restaurants. In the first situation, I was in a restaurant and ordered a meal, and when they brought it out, they had messed up the order. When I pointed out that they messed it up, an agitated waiter took the plate and stormed back into the kitchen. Ten minutes later, the waiter brought out the new food without so much as an apology. The second situation was similar in that they brought out the food, only this time it didn't really taste like what I had expected, and when the pleasant server asked how my food was, I told her it wasn't what I was expecting, she immediately offered to get me something else and even made a couple of suggestions. As they were preparing the new order, a manager came over and apologized and said they would not be charging me for my food and would get me dessert as well.

In the second example, the restaurant turned what I call a negative to a positive, and I can guarantee I'll go back to that restaurant and recommend it to others. The first restaurant doesn't have a chance of seeing me again.

There will always be mistakes made in any business because people are human; it's how you deal with those mistakes and how you turn negatives to positives that are critical to your business and your profitability. You should be training your team on how to deal with mistakes and customer issues, and also give them the ability to make customer decisions on the spot to make a customer happy without taking the customer through bureaucracy just for the sake of it. This will position you and your team to turn negatives into positives. And I guarantee that this will add to your profitability!

Word of Mouth

Word of mouth can be the most important form of marketing you can do, and word of mouth is only accomplished through great customer service and great products and services. And today, with technology, word of mouth takes on a whole new meaning. From Twitter to Facebook to apps like Yelp, you can create word of mouth almost instantly. By encouraging your customers to engage in those tools, you can immediately build word of mouth through great customer service. Asking your customers to spread the word when they get great service and to tell you when they don't is essential. The flip side to that, though, is that customers will typically share a negative experience much more often than they will share a positive experience.

One of the most important aspects of this is that it's a strategy, not just something that happens. Clearly write out what you want to happen and then share that with your team and determine how you can best spread word of mouth. Make sure your team understands the technology tools that you are using and encourage them to participate in the conversations. By developing this strategy, you not only encourage exceptional service but also ramp up your marketing efforts.

Off Boarding

One of the most important things all business owners need to do is to let go of the things they don't do well and have someone else do them. Off Boarding is passing on things you don't do well to someone else outside of your organization. Whether that's accounting, legal, administration or marketing functions, if you don't do it well, hand it off to someone else that will do it well. Most entrepreneurs that I've dealt with over the years have a tendency to be control freaks, and they want their hands in everything. What they don't understand is that control is holding back their business. There are others inside and outside the business that can do some of those functions much better and more efficiently than they can, and it allows the entrepreneur to focus on what they do best. This is one of the most difficult things entrepreneurs do, but when they do it, they exponentially grow their businesses because it allows them to clearly focus on what they do best and what the business needs them to do. I have had many clients over the years, and in my own business where I didn't want to do financials, it is the one thing I hate doing but obviously a very necessary component to a business. When I found the right financial person that could take those things off my plate and do them for me, I was able to focus on the things that I liked doing and was good at doing and let him input the financials and create reports that I could then use to assess where my business was. This was the best offboarding I could do.

Leverage Relationships

In this strategy, we look at how you can leverage existing relationships that you may have with other businesses. A good example of this would be utilizing a particular group of prospective customers you are currently working with that has a similar need to another company that offers an ancillary product or service with which you have a relationship. A great example here is a financial services company I've worked with that has advisors who utilize my services but also need to sell a financial product that another one of my clients sells. So I have introduced my clients to this other company as a way of enhancing their business. This isn't so much a referral as it is doing business by association. If you can tell the story that you're working with one member of a group, it can lead to multiple relationships within that same group.

The best thing to do to implement this is to inventory your customers to see who is involved in a group. It could be the same company, an industry group or a trade group. Then determine how you let them know you already have one of them as a customer. Getting a great testimonial from that one customer will also be a great way to get into that group.

Parallel Opportunities

Parallel opportunities simply mean finding other similar businesses looking to expand their businesses and then working together with each other's customer lists. For example, I work with a chiropractor, and with this strategy, we are working with a fitness store, a massage therapy business and a salon/spa. We have put together a marketing campaign where they promote each other's businesses with events, online marketing and email marketing. This strategy has been very beneficial to each other's growth.

One important note about this strategy, it is vital for this to work that you find partners that are willing to execute the marketing and participate equally. If you can find those parallel markets and businesses, this can be a very profitable strategy. You will want to create a letter of agreement or understanding on what each one will do and what the expectations are on the front end. You want to review the relationship occasionally so that everyone feels they are equally benefitting from the strategy and agreement.

Business strategies are important to execute at all times, but in times of crisis, they are even more important. The strategies that you execute should be in line with the purpose, mission and guiding principles of your organization, as a disconnect can do more harm than good. Pursuing a strategy that flies in the face of your purpose can lead to disaster, especially during a crisis.

Questions for thought

1. Is your organization strategic or does it chase after the latest and greatest tactics without any overriding strategy?

2. Do you employ multiple strategies? If so, what are they?

3. What are your strengths, and do you dedicate the bulk of your time to them?

4. Have you looked at all possible ways to generate revenue, especially to ways that may be outside the standard strategies done in your industry?

CHAPTER 6
Principled Selling

Approach each customer with the idea
of helping them solve a problem or
achieve a goal, not sell a product.

—Zig Ziglar

Over the last thirty years, much of the work I've done has been with sales organizations, training and coaching over three thousand salespeople. I see selling as a noble profession and vital to the success of an organization, yet many times salespeople are looked at in a negative light. They are depicted as pushy, aggressive, dishonest, sneaky and lacking integrity. Salespeople face many negative perceptions about their work, and how they react to these perceptions ultimately will determine their success. Most sales training and development focus on better tactics and strategies to overcome the perceptions. There is a better way to address these perceptions, and it is called principled selling. It helps address how you work and how to turn your work into work well done. Unfortunately, salespeople themselves, in many cases, have been their own worst enemies by the methods they use, and organizations have encouraged this by the way they train and manage salespeople. They train salespeople using highly questionable tactics.

One of my favorite movies is *Glengarry Glen Ross*, about real estate salespeople. In the movie, David Mamet introduces us to a world of success and failure of salesmen in real estate, which, in effect, is a microcosm of the reality of the USA. He presents a world in which the salesmen are dominated by the fact that they need to close the leads; otherwise, they lose their jobs. This is a world of corrupt values where people are prepared to tread on others in order to help themselves. Their love of money is so great that they become selfish, devious, materialistic and extremely competitive. It especially judges success and failure by how you close (ABC Always Be Closing) and how you win. This portrayal is all too familiar in sales organizations today. There is a better way, and it starts with the definition of selling.

In *Webster's Dictionary*, the definition of selling is defined as "selling is providing goods and/or services for the exchange of money." This is a very simplistic view of selling. A better definition for selling is the exchange of ideas and concepts between people who provide solutions to problems and basic needs and to make people feel better. Just about any product or service can fit in this description, but the main point of this definition is that selling is about people. It's about the exchange of ideas and concepts to get people to think about their problems, circumstances or wants and needs and then provide a solution to address them. If we start with people in the selling equation, then it reframes the whole process. When we recognize the human person as salespeople, it should reframe the whole process of training and developing salespeople.

The Interior Work of Selling

Most sales training programs start with exterior work, meaning how the salesperson presents, overcomes objections, and offers products and services. However, if we start with the idea that we need to develop people from the inside first, this opens up a whole new possibility of creating successful salespeople. Interior work focuses on the person themselves and is the by-product, the trailing indicator of serving a mission bigger than yourself. If we develop people that fit the mission and purpose of the organization, we can create successful patterns.

In all my years of working with hundreds of salespeople, I have used some of the concepts I'll be sharing and have seen great results for salespeople and organizations. The interior work of selling begins with the idea of character, or what Alexander Havard, author of *The Virtuous Leader*, calls the "content of character." He goes on to say, "it is virtue or more precisely the set of classical human virtues, above all magnanimity, humility, prudence, courage, self-control and justice." Havard speaks about these qualities for leaders, and I believe that these same virtues apply to salespeople.

Virtues can be developed by habits over time that are not intrinsic to the human person. This isn't a new concept. In Stephen Covey's book *The Seven Habits of Highly Effective People*, he undertook the study of success literature in the US since 1776. Here's what he found, "The success literature for the past fifty years was superficial, filled with techniques and quick fixes, with social Band-Aids and aspirin. In stark contrast, almost all of the literature in the first two hundred years or so focused on what could be called the Character Ethic as the foundation of success—things like integrity, humility, simplicity, modesty, and The Golden Rule. Thus, in a little over a generation, we have largely abandoned the enduring character qualities that shaped our history." What are these virtues, and why are they important to salespeople? Here are the key sales virtues and what they have the ability to do:

> **Prudence:** to make right decisions.
>
> **Courage:** to stay the course and resist pressures of all kinds.
>
> **Self-Control:** to maintain focus on the mission at hand and avoid distractions of all sorts.
>
> **Justice:** to give every individual his own due and to treat others the way you want to be treated.
>
> **Magnanimity:** to strive for great things, to challenge myself and others.
>
> **Humility:** to be a humble servant and overcome selfishness and serve others.

Building virtue into sales development takes longer. The organization must exercise radical patience in developing salespeople, coaching them and nurturing them. But the results mean more engaged, loyal salespeople who become successful for the right reasons and always put the mission and purpose of the organization first and their customers and their reasons for being customers second. Salespeople are developed to make conscious decisions based on how they impact these two. This becomes a win for the organization, the customer, and ultimately for the salesperson.

The Why of Selling

I started by stating the definition of selling is people exchanging ideas, but in order to do that, there must be a defined purpose for the organization or, at the very least, a defined purpose of the salesperson. There are many salespeople who work for companies that do not have a purpose and mission, but that doesn't mean they can't have one; they can develop their purpose and mission.

In Simon Sinek's book *Start with Why* he introduces the idea of The Golden Circle, and in this representation, he creates a circle with three rings, the outside ring is the "What," the middle ring is the "How" and the inside ring is the "Why." He states how most organizations talk about what they do from the outside in starting with what they do, how they do it and why they do it. However, there are transformational organizations such as Apple that start from the inside out. They start with why they exist, why they get out of bed every morning, and why should anyone care? In starting there and then defining how they create the products they create and what they are, they have truly put themselves ahead of other companies that do the exact same thing as Apple.

Defining your "why" is critical to your sales success. Our "why" should be our purpose, cause or belief. It is a way to not only differentiate yourself but also your organization on a completely different playing field from competitors. Most organizations start with what they do and how they do it and completely miss the "why" they do what they do. Defining your why also ties directly into defining your purpose. For salespeople, it's important to not only have the organizational purpose, but you should also have your own personal purpose, what gets you out of bed in the morning to strive for success and how it interplays into the organizational purpose.

Sell like a Monk

As I stated in an earlier chapter, the Rule of Benedict might be called the rule of listening. The very first word of the rule is listen. The art of listening is not just about hearing someone, but it's the ability to step outside oneself and focus on the person you're listening to. It's about setting aside ego and the desire to sell something and focusing on the person's real needs. In other words, being attuned to the person you're listening to. The Rule of Benedict also gives us principles that can build and enhance salespeople. Those principles from the Rule can be put in the context of sales as follows:

Creating Trust

To be successful, you must be able to persuade people to do things that satisfy their needs and wants and purchase solutions that you recommend. However, in order to persuade, you must first create trust. One of the ways Benedict talks about creating trust is through becoming disinterested and detached. What he means by that is that the person listening puts themselves and their self-interests aside and completely engages in the person they are listening to. They are not trying to be a step ahead with their next response. A trustworthy person is selfless, and service is at the core of their being. One of the few TV shows I watch is called New Amsterdam, and it's about a public hospital in New York that brings in a new medical director. In his first meeting with the staff, he asks the question, "How can I help you?" He then allows them to give him ideas, crazy or not, about what they can change. By creating trust, they know that he will respectfully listen to the idea and, if possible, figure out what to do about it.

Focus on Excellence

When I write about excellence, it's not enough just to be good at selling your products and services; it's how you live your work. It's a complete commitment to quality. Aristotle recognized the nature of excellence as a virtue. He characterized it as something that stems from habitual practice—we are what we repeatedly do. Benedict tells his monks that after working the steps required of humility, good habit and delight in virtue will come effortlessly. What seemed impossible or extremely difficult in the beginning will gradually give inexpressible delight if they stay on task. Excellence should be focused on for the sake of excellence, not just doing well. The monastic method is a focus on doing excellence rather than being excellent.

Building Community

The profession of selling and the success or failure of it not only lies on the individual salesperson but on a whole community of people involved with that salesperson. It includes management, co-workers, customer service, finance, vendors and a wealth of others inside the community, as well as those supporting the salesperson at home. When Benedict speaks of community, it is one of the most important tenets of the Rule. In laying out the specifics about community, he talks of respect, patience, openness and action. In sales, we work in a wide community, and if we are to be successful, we must understand that same relationship that Benedict talks about in the community. We respect those that we work with; we have patience when things aren't going the way they should be, and we are open and caring of others. And we must act and not just talk about these things; our actions must be performing good works and virtuous living. The way we treat customers as part of our community is essential to our success, and by practicing community in the way Benedict wrote about, we create vibrant, flourishing work.

Stability

The idea of stability in Benedict's world was wedded in maturity. By having a fixed point that one is able to mature. In today's world of changing jobs constantly, we have lost some of this stability. The grass is always greener on the other side, and so we seek out a perceived better deal. We see this in salespeople more so than maybe any other profession. However, if our work is experienced as a calling, and we take the time to develop our inner self, stability helps us acknowledge that all personal change happens from the inside out. If we create a sense of stability or loyalty to one's self first and understand that change is constant and in sales, we will constantly have ups and downs, but if we are true to ourselves and continue to develop our inner sales game, then it will allow us to do work well. The Rule of Benedict covers many areas of organizational life and, if read and studied closely, can be a watershed of ideas in many different areas of selling. At its heart, it talks about the way we treat others with dignity and respect, and by starting there, we come at sales from a different perspective.

What Do We Sell?

Unfortunately, most sales organizations view what they sell as products or services, and there is nothing further from the truth. Most salespeople sell on three concepts, price, product or performance. Their product is either cheaper than the competitor, it's better or unique, or it will outdo the competitor in some way. When I would train financial advisors in these aspects, I would tell them that if you are selling on these three concepts, you will eventually lose. Someone will always be cheaper, have a better product or service or outperform you. So is there a better way to sell? What salespeople should be selling is value, solutions and peace of mind. In looking at these three concepts, you are now drilling down to what the customer is really looking for, what is their perceived value, what problem or need are they trying to solve, and what will give them peace of mind and/or happiness. The sales process must be redesigned to focus on these areas, and that is especially critical in times of crisis. Understanding the customers' needs is even more important during those times.

Sales Training vs. Sales Development

Many sales organizations have spent countless millions of dollars putting on programs to train their sales teams. And certainly, many sales training companies and individuals have made countless millions providing these programs. These programs go back to the early days of sales training, which were primarily geared toward motivation, and then into the technical side of sales training with the programs developed by Xerox and IBM. Then tweaked or changed into programs developed for other specific industries. Programs then evolved into what I call the intellectual side of selling, which sprung from books like *Conceptual Selling* and *Strategic Selling*. Sales trainers and motivational speakers have been a constant in the sales business since Dale Carnegie, and companies have engaged these trainers with the hope that they could help their sales teams find that magic bullet that would take them to the next level.

The Focus of Sales Training

Sales training has primarily been focused on four core areas:

1. Selling Skills
2. Product Training

3. Industry Training

4. Company-Specific Training

According to the American Society of Training and Development (ASTD), this training accounts for virtually 95 percent of all sales training done in organizations. Selling skills account for one-third of that training, with product training a close second. The interesting part of this training is the most popular approach used in delivering it is the classroom approach, and the least popular is the coaching and in-field support.

In another study, it was reported that US businesses spend $15 billion per year on sales training and an average of $2,000 per salesperson. However, most of those salespeople find the training ineffective or less than useful. One of the primary reasons they found it ineffective is that it didn't get top-down support from higher-level management, and it wasn't carried forward into the field and implemented within their sales plans. And most of the training is a reactive approach to competitive markets and is focused on the transaction.

A Different Approach: The Sales Development and Planning Model

Sales development and planning look at the entire process of selling and focuses on the key areas that are critical to the success of the salesperson. Once we have identified the areas that are holding them back, we then use a very specific process of creating a strategic action plan that will focus on those areas and break them into bite-sized pieces that can be easily implemented. And then, we will take it "into the field" and help them execute the plan through a coaching process.

The six areas of critical focus are:

1. Maximizing Productivity

2. Personal Branding and Marketing

3. Understanding and Executing the Sales Process

4. Uncovering Opportunities and Growing Your Sales

5. Delivering Exceptional Service

6. Building and Keeping Relationships

These six areas represent thirty years of study and working with thousands of salespeople to determine what areas impact their sales and how they impact their sales. These areas differ from standard sales training in that they are strategic; they focus on executing what they have learned in the sales training they have already received. They are highly customizable, meaning every salesperson has things they do better or worse. By identifying the areas that they are struggling with, we can assist them in creating a plan that will be their plan, not some cookie-cutter approach that everyone has. By taking salespeople through a series of exercises, we can help them pinpoint the issues holding them back, and then we can go to work on building a plan to help them strengthen those areas. We may find that part of their issues may be that they need to go back through some part of the sales training process, and that's where this approach dovetails into the programs companies have already implemented.

Sales is one of the most critical aspects of any organization. Without customers, you don't have an organization. Rethinking the way sales are done, especially during a crisis, helped many clients I worked with during the financial crisis survive and thrive.

Questions For Thought

1. Does your sales process involve value, solutions and peace of mind?

2. Does your sales training focus on soft skills like humility?

3. Does sales excellence in your organization include connecting back to your purpose?

4. Do you hire based on character versus talent?

CHAPTER 7
Thriving in a Crisis: Innovation and The Possibility Wheel

We cannot solve our problems using the same thinking we used when we created them.

—Albert Einstein

In March of 2020, the world shut down. An outbreak of COVID-19 in China started a domino effect that reached around the globe, impacting nearly every person. Life as we knew it stopped, no working together, no going out for dinner or a movie, no family get-togethers, and we had to take care of each other remotely via Zoom. In addition, financial markets crashed, and there was great uncertainty. But very soon after March, scientists began frantically working on how to slow the virus down and how to prevent it. They began to work on vaccines, and the urgency created a scientific community across the world with one sole purpose, to knock this virus out. It doesn't matter whether you're for or against vaccines; the facts are that almost an entire scientific community was involved in dealing with change through the innovation process. In addition to the scientific community, the rest of us were also trying to figure out what the world would look like and how we would function. From big corporations to Mom and Pop businesses, all were trying to figure out how to survive this crisis. As I saw in the financial crisis of 2008, drastic change would be the tipping point to innovation—businesses and all organizations and institutions had to innovate to manage the change. Some did it much better than others, and the process they used, whether deliberate or by accident, allowed them to survive and even thrive as the pandemic carried on for over two years.

I remember talking to a friend of mine that owns several restaurants. They had to completely shut down for the first two months of the crisis, but then the challenge became how do we reopen safely and how do we conduct business. They had very little take-out business before the pandemic and now had systems in place to handle take-out. In addition, they had an extensive wine inventory that was for customers dining in. They quickly implemented a take-out system and rotated their employees in and out so everyone was getting hours. They alerted their customers that you could still get the same great food and eat it in the safety of your home. And they put their wine on sale so that people could pick up a bottle of wine and take it home to have with their dinner. During holiday seasons, they created full dinner menus that people could pick up for the entire family. When they looked at the numbers after the first year of the pandemic, they had actually held their own even after being completely shut down for two months. In the second year, as people were allowed back into the restaurant, they continued the take-out service and wine sale, and in year two, they thrived. During a time when many restaurants had gone out of business, they faced the change by innovating and adapting to the world around them.

Thinking Differently

When people face a crisis, one of the biggest challenges to overcome the crisis is the ability to think differently. A crisis situation creates stress, and when faced with stress, we naturally retreat to thinking about how we get back to where we were. Instead, we need to be thinking about new ways to get out ahead of the crisis and new methods of doing business that we maybe haven't thought about before. In order to do that, we need to think differently. In Adam Grants' book, *Think Again*, he says, "…in a turbulent world, there's another set of cognitive skills that might matter more; the ability to rethink and unlearn." As COVID began to shut the world down, I can remember having conversations with some of my coaching clients and what they were trying to do was to use the old crisis playbook that said you basically dig in and weather out the storm. The problem with this thinking is that there really was no playbook for COVID. We didn't know what the long-term implications were going to be and what the impact was. We were living in what the US military refers to as "VUCA"—volatile, uncertain, complex and ambiguous conditions. So the old playbook wasn't going to work, and it not only wasn't going to work, it was completely irrelevant. To get through the crisis, we had to rethink and unlearn what we were going to do and what we thought we knew.

Rethinking starts with understanding how we think. In *Think Again*, Adam Grant talks about the three ways that we typically think. He calls them the preacher, prosecutor and politician. Here's how he describes them, "We go into preacher mode when our sacred beliefs are in jeopardy, we deliver sermons to protect and promote our ideals. We enter prosecutor mode when we recognize flaws in other people's reasoning: we marshal arguments to prove them wrong and win our case. We shift into politician mode when we're seeking to win over an audience; we campaign and lobby for the approval of our constitution. The risk is that we become so wrapped up in preaching that we're right, prosecuting others who are wrong and politicking for support that we don't bother to rethink our own views." When I take people through an exercise in rethinking in my workshops, I first have them identify an area where they have thought in one or more of these three ways, and in almost every case, the first example that comes out is with their children. We are constantly using one of these three methods. I do it with my four-year-old grandson. First, I try to convince him of the value of my idea, and when he argues about it, I tell him you need to do whatever it is we're talking about, and of course, when that fails, I try to win him over, and that usually requires a snack of some sort.

In order to think differently, we need what Grant calls "a different pair of goggles." We need to think like a scientist. To think like a scientist means that we are constantly aware of our limits of understanding. There are four steps to this type of rethinking. First, we need to doubt everything we know. As both the financial crisis and the COVID pandemic raged, we were required to doubt the old solutions and old playbooks because they simply were not going to work. The second step to rethinking was to become inquisitive and start looking at other ideas and researching other potential ways of overcoming the obstacles. By becoming curious, we uncover new ways of doing things. The third step to rethinking is one right out of The Rule of Benedict that I talked about in an earlier chapter, and that is humility. When we realize that we don't know everything and don't have all the answers, then we open up new possibilities. Benedict believed this was the most important aspect of living and working in the community. When we accomplish these three steps, it leads to the last step, which is the discovery of new ideas, new ways of doing things and, potentially, solutions for the crisis we're involved in. In my workshops, I have people pick a problem they're dealing with and begin to think differently with the ground rule that they can't come up with anything that has been done in the past. It's very interesting to watch because when you add that ground rule, it suddenly takes the blinders off, and they can really start being creative in how they address the problem.

Crisis and Innovation

During the financial crisis of 2008 and the pandemic, we saw numerous examples of innovation that resulted from the crisis. I remember working with financial services firms in 2008 and 2009 and helping them quickly pivot from selling products to offering education and support to their clients. And certainly, we can look at the things that have happened during COVID, such as vaccines and new ways of doing business and education remotely that are a direct result of innovative thinking. What are the drivers of innovation during a crisis? First is a sense of urgency. During COVID, I worked with two clients that, had they not come up with new innovative ideas, would have gone out of business. So there was a very real sense of urgency that pushed them into innovative thinking. Second, there is a commitment to resources. In times of crisis, long-term projects and expenditures typically lose out to more urgent needs, and therefore, resources are directed to those needs. Be it people or money or equipment, the resources are available when in normal times, they may not be. And lastly, there is an openness to new ideas. With my clients during the financial crisis, I saw a very definite shift from selling as much as we could to taking care of our clients, and with that shift came a completely new set of ideas that hadn't even been thought about before. Innovation happens during a crisis, which is very similar to how it happens during a startup. The startup is typically facing a VUCA environment, and therefore in order for this new business to be successful, it's vital to have innovation to be successful. In the fourteen different startups I've been involved in, it was essential that innovation happen. When it didn't happen, failure occurred. I've learned more from the six failures I've had than from the eight successes because you realize where you failed in the innovation process, and you try not to make the same mistakes as you did before.

The Possibility Wheel

In order to develop innovation and innovative ideas, we should not have to rely on a crisis. It should be a constant state of development for every organization. The Possibility Wheel is a tool I developed to help clients work through the process of innovation. This tool takes you through a process from start to finish; however, it's important to note that it's a continual process. Like a wheel, it continues to turn, always in motion.

The first step to the wheel is to develop an environment that encourages rethinking, in teams, in meetings, in product development, in marketing and everywhere in the organization. Make thinking like a scientist the norm, so people constantly doubt what they know, being curious about what else is possible, being humble in not knowing it all and then finding a discovery.

The second step to the wheel is to initiate. This is to have a process to filter all the ideas that come from rethinking. I have helped clients create innovation teams, and their primary role is to determine what ideas are executable and then put a process in place to do them. The initiate process is all about creating bite-sized ideas that can be executed, measured and scaled. The next three steps of the wheel follow.

Execution is the most important step on the wheel. There have been many great ideas that never happened because no one executed them. The most important piece of this execution is to create it in bite-sized pieces. In the lean startup world, they call them minimally viable products or MVPs. This bite-sized idea, or MVP, requires three things. First, it must require a minimum amount of time to create—speed is of the essence. Second, it must take a few resources to create, and third, it must be measurable. In *The Lean Startup*, Eric Ries says of the MVP, "it requires a full turn…with a minimum amount of effort and the least amount of development."

The fourth step is to measure the idea. As the idea is created, we need to be able to implement ways to measure it to see if it works and if it achieves what we want it to achieve. Whether it's a product that sells, a process that makes us more efficient or a method that solves a problem, there must be a way to measure it in some form. That measurement needs to occur throughout the process, not just at the end.

The fifth step is to scale, that is, to build it out from an MVP to a complete product, service, method, process or way of doing business. During COVID, the group of restaurants I mentioned earlier went from just doing take-out to creating entire family menus and holiday dinners for take-out. That was a method of scaling their MVP.

After the fifth step, it may be time to rethink the idea to improve it or it may be time to pivot altogether because the MVP didn't work and come up with a new MVP that solves the problem.

A Real-Life MVP

I have the privilege of working with members of the Sioux Falls Police Department, and through that work, I learned about an officer working in one of the more challenging schools in the city. Each morning he passed a girl in the hallway. She was always downcast, didn't make eye contact and rarely said hello even though he said hello to her. One day she was joyous and engaging. It caught him by surprise, so he asked her why she was so happy. She said she just got her hair done and was so excited by that. He went home that night and had a conversation with his wife. Could something that simple bring that much joy? And if so, was there something he could do to help other kids experience that? He and his wife came up with a simple idea of getting a couple of salons she knew of to kick in a couple of free hair appointments. Then he huddled with the school counselors to see who might be a good candidate for this. He also then thought that maybe along with the haircut, he should take them out to lunch at a sit-down restaurant as many of these kids had never had anything but fast food. He then took it a step further and got one of the local retailers to kick in a gift card and he took the student shopping that same day. They could buy new shoes, a new outfit, whatever they wanted with the gift card. To make a long story short, the program became very successful and began with both a boy and a girl each month. The mayor got wind of the program and issued a commendation to the officer, and within two years, the police department was doing the program in many of the city's schools. The officer had an idea. He figured out an MVP (the haircut), he measured and scaled the MVP (lunch and a shopping trip), and then the program got even more scaling with the city-wide launch. The officer started this process by rethinking, doubting what he knew about the girl, finding out more about her and why she was so happy and being humble to ask his wife the question, is this really a big deal? And that led to the discovery of an MVP that was executed. This was one of the very cool stories I learned about in my work and it had a great impact, which I'll talk about in the next chapter.

Questions For Thought

1. Is there a current problem or situation that you face where you can practice the process of rethinking?

2. How has your organization changed and adapted to the pandemic?

3. Is there an idea that you have or that those on your team have that an MVP could be created from?

4. From that MVP idea, can you create a plan that would initiate it, execute it and measure it?

CHAPTER 8
The Flourishing Organization:
From Success to Impact

In the end, it is about Truly caring for
every precious human being whose
life we touch. It is about including
everybody, not just the fortunate few or
the exceptionally talented. It is about
living with an abundance mindset; and
abundance of patience, love, hope, and
opportunity. Everyone wants to contribute.
Trust them. Leaders are everywhere.

—Bob Chapman, *Everybody Matters*

Were the organizations that didn't survive the financial crisis asleep at the wheel? NO! But what they were doing was fighting the last war. They were doing business the way they always did business, no different than the Sears and Kmarts of the world, caught off guard by Walmart and Amazon. The organizations that survived and especially thrived during the crisis understood how to do business differently, and they did things with intent. Those organizations that I call Flourishing Organizations zigged when everyone else zagged and had their teams on board to do that. I discovered certain principles that those successful companies did and in today's world must do so that they don't get caught fighting "past wars."

In looking back at the companies I worked with during the financial crisis and the pandemic, those companies that survived and thrived put many of these principles to work. They may not have had this written in a document somewhere; however, they operated under these principles. It's what allowed them to come out of the crisis strong and helped them become even stronger after the crisis. These principles also led them from being successful to having a great impact on the lives of their employees, their customers and other stakeholders and in their communities. Let's take a look at each of these principles.

What does it mean to be a Flourishing Organization? First, let's examine the word intentional. The dictionary says the meaning of intentional is to do something deliberate and with purpose. It also says to do something with the end in mind. So as we look at what a Flourishing Organization is, based on the definition, it means that it is an organization that does things on purpose and deliberately with the end in mind. The Flourishing Organization does the things they do, understanding that what they do will impact all those who come into contact with it, including employees, customers and communities. With that in mind, I've laid out six guiding beliefs that organizations must pursue to be considered a Flourishing Organization. These guiding principles cover many of the points I have discussed in previous chapters, and these guiding principles were observed as I worked with clients during the financial crises. And in fact, by executing these principles, many of them thrived during that time. The Flourishing Organization is based on these six guiding principles:

1. Virtue, Strengths Based Leadership

2. Positive, Purpose-Driven Culture

3. Driven by Innovation

4. Higher Purpose that Fosters Common Good

5. Adaptable to Deep Change

6. Long-Term Viability/Profitability

Virtue, Strengths Based Leadership

Doing the right thing. This seems to be such a simple phrase, but how many times have we seen just the opposite in organizations. St. Thomas Aquinas said, "happiness is secured through virtue; it is a good attained by man's own will." Virtue and virtuous behavior by the leaders of organizations create flourishing environments. Character is exercising virtue, and if leaders understand their character strengths and use those strengths in balance, they create the soil for the entire organization to flourish. However, if they do not act with virtue and character, they themselves can take down an entire organization, and we've seen plenty of examples of that in the corporate world. In order to have a Flourishing Organization, it must first start with the leaders exercising virtue.

Positive, Purpose-Driven Culture

The organization that understands its "why" and how it integrates that "why" into its culture is the first principle. Without this principle, the others below cannot exist. In the book *Conscious Capitalism*, John Mackey and Raj Sisodia say this about purpose, "Purpose is most powerful when it taps into a universal human truth. In other words, it is fully aligned with the higher aspects of what it means to be human (or, as Abraham Lincoln eloquently put it, with the better angels of our nature). Such a purpose has an uplifting moral quality, appealing to people's highest ideals and motives and transcending their own personal concerns." Purpose coupled with a positive culture brings out the best in people. When leaders exercise positive behaviors such as gratitude, forgiveness, humility and listening, they create positive energy, and that energy creates an environment of human flourishing. The statistics have shown that these organizations that embrace purpose and create a positive culture and have a foundation of a virtuousness of character take the first step to becoming a Flourishing Organization.

A positive culture is also one that is responsible to stakeholders and means that stakeholders come first; profits come second. Treating employees, customers, vendors and the community with dignity and respect is the key element of the principle. Allowing decision-making to happen at all levels of the organization shows responsibility to stakeholders and not just lip service. Being responsible to stakeholders also means that products and services add value to customers and that the broader community can be enhanced by the Flourishing Organization. The companies that do this will ultimately find that even though profitability comes second, it is still very profitable to operate this way.

Driven by Innovation

The Flourishing Organization doesn't just react to a crisis with innovation; it is constantly innovating in all the ways it goes about its business. It has created an environment that fosters rethinking so that everyone from the front desk to the corner office, factory floor to the conference rooms are doubting what they know, asking questions and being curious, exercising humility that says they don't know it all and then discovering new ideas that can lead to innovation. They don't let the ideas sit; they leap into action with them and execute them, measure and scale them. And most importantly, they are constantly doing this.

Higher Purpose that Fosters the Common Good

The Flourishing Organization creates goods and services that benefit those who use them, and in providing those goods, it also takes some of the profits from selling those goods and services and gives them back to the community they serve. So they have a bigger mission than just their customers and shareholders. When they add in higher purpose that is not measured by economic output but by contributions to society, they foster common good. Creating higher purpose must start with a vision and purpose that clearly defines the organization and then create from that vision. Creating goods and services takes resources, including capital, environmental resources and human capital. The Flourishing Organization realizes that these are limited, not finite resources, and therefore, they are good stewards for long-term sustainability. They are also supportive of the stewardship of all resources in light of the common good. The document "The Vocation of The Business Leader" states, "Rather, the Christian business leader serves the common good by creating goods that are truly good and services that truly serve. The goods and services that businesses produce should meet authentic human needs, so they include not only things with clear social value such as life-saving medical devices, microfinance, education, social investment, fair trade products, renewable energy, artistic enterprises, healthcare, or affordable housing but also anything that genuinely contributes to human development."

Adaptability to Deep Change

Change is inevitable, and the Flourishing Organization understands that and thrives on it. When a crisis occurs, they shift into high gear and are ready for the change needed to adapt. In Robert Quinn's book, *Deep Change* he says, "Deep change differs from incremental change in that it requires new ways of thinking and behaving. It is change that is major in scope, discontinuous with the past and generally irreversible. That deep change effort distorts existing patterns of action and involves taking risks. Deep change means surrendering control." For most people and organizations, change is uncomfortable, and therefore, the uncertainty that can accompany it is difficult. However, Flourishing Organizations and their leaders understand that in order to thrive, change must happen, and it can't just be what Quinn called incremental change. It has to be deep change. These leaders also understand that this isn't some knee-jerk reaction, but there is a definite process to deep change that brings people along positively and doesn't create chaos in the organization. It's also important to note that part of that process is to get people engaged as early as possible and to give people decision-making ability at the lowest level, that principle of subsidiarity that I talked about in an earlier chapter. When people come on board, and the deep change is engaging, everyone then flourishing happens.

Long-Term Viability/Profitability

To accomplish the first five guiding principles, the Flourishing Organization must be profitable in order to stay in business. Thinking strategically, not tactically, and executing strategies for long-term, stable growth is essential to the organization. Tying strategy back to purpose and mission assures long-term success. As St. Benedict knew, people will come and go, but if a system is created that focuses on long-term viability, the organization will stand.

For leaders of organizations to lead well and create Flourishing Organizations, they must create an environment of safety, where employees know that the organization has their back and can do their jobs and give their input without worrying about the consequences. Leaders that create that type of environment also create trust and cooperation, which are essential attributes of the Flourishing Organization. In Simon Sinek's book *The Infinite Game*, he says, "The responsibility of business is to use its will and resources to advance a cause greater than itself, protect the people and places in which they operate and generate more resources so that it can continue doing all those things for as long as possible. An organization can do whatever it likes to build its business so long as it is responsible for the consequences of its actions." One last thing regarding Flourishing Organizations, they are not necessarily businesses or large organizations. They could be teams or departments. Anywhere a group of people is working for a common purpose can be a Flourishing Organization.

From Success to Impact

I've had the opportunity to work with hundreds of organizations over the last thirty-plus years, and many of those organizations were very successful. However, they measured success be it profits, market share, stock price, customers, members, donors, whatever the measuring stick was, they were successful. But in all this work that I've done, as I reflect back on the financial crisis of 2008 and the pandemic of the last few years, many of the successful organizations that I worked with still struggled in those crises. However, there were a few organizations that not only survived those times but also thrived, and

I think the biggest difference is that those organizations were much more concerned with impact, not success. They knew that if they operated from the baseline of making an impact on their people, their stakeholders, their community and society in general, and they did it in a way that respected the dignity of all people, they were able to flourish even in a crisis. As we come out of the pandemic, we are now dealing with what's being called the Great Resignation and supply chain issues and high inflation, not to mention political and societal devisiveness; there can be no greater call for leaders and organizations to operate for impact and not success. I believe that in order for our country and the world to overcome these issues, we must do the right thing, exercise human dignity, be kind, open our minds and listen to all sides, exercise humility, and trust that God has a plan and it's a good plan, we just have to let it work and do our part. If people and organizations operate in this light, they will find their Sweet Spot. In this revision of this book, I've tried to lay out my reflections on what I saw during the financial crisis of 2008–09 and the pandemic; in addition, I've tried to add insights into those reflections based on considerable research. Ultimately, you, the reader, will be the judge of what was accomplished. However, if I have given you a few nuggets of ideas, information or principles that you can put to work so that the company you lead, the organization you direct or the team you manage can be better tomorrow than it is today, then I have accomplished what I set out to do. I wish you all the best in finding your Sweet Spot and hitting your work and your life square on the face of the club and looking up and saying, "Wow, that felt great!"

Acknowledgments

Since I first published *Sweet Spot* on my own and then had it picked up by Calumet Editions to be published under its Wisdom Editions imprint, we've been through a pandemic, civil and political unrest and now war in Europe. Some things have changed for the better, and some for the worse. When Calumet Editions approached me about doing a revised edition of *The Sweet Spot,* I began looking at what could be updated and changed and where my own personal experiences could enhance this revised edition. I've added additional thoughts on both the financial crisis of 2008 as well as the current crisis we face. I continue to be blessed in my work at the Benedictine Leadership Institute at Mount Marty University and the individuals and organizations that I get to work with both through that work and through my own business, Principled Flourishing Group. Here then is the revised edition of *The Sweet Spot: Where Business Strategy, Positive Psychology and Faith Principles Converge.*

    The writing of this book has taken many turns over the past three years. It has been written and re-written several times, but it really took flight when I started taking my experiences, knowledge and reflections and combining them with the research and development of the Certificate of Integrated Leadership program at Mount Marty University. It has been a true blessing to be involved and direct that project. It allowed me to incorporate principles that I felt needed to be in this book.

Many people have had a direct influence on this book and on my journey over thirty years in business. First, my clients, who, over the years, have helped me learn way more than I ever taught them. Second, to my friend and colleague Joe Rutten, whose vision and energy keep me going. To Jason Heron and Marc Long at Mount Marty University, who have helped me and supported me in developing the Certificate of Integrated Leadership. Without their wisdom, insight and support, this could not have happened—also, Dr. Tom Lorang, my sounding board, offered his guidance through this project. To the rest of the advisory team from the certificate program: Larry Canfield, Noel Lais and Chad Eckroth, who challenged us to think outside the box.

Most importantly, I couldn't have finished this without Anne, my best friend, my cheerleader, and whom I get to travel this journey hand in hand. You are my sweet spot! And to Karin, Ellen, James and Kyle, who keep cheering me on and have been the most pleasant surprise blessing I could have ever imagined. And finally, to Steve, Dave and Pat. Your friendship through all the years and your experiences helped create the idea behind this book. I look forward to our many more years to come!

List of Resources

Vocation of the Business Leader: A Reflection, Dicastery for Promoting Integral Human Development.

Bennis, Warren, *On Becoming a Leader*.

Blanchard, Ken, *Raving Fans*.

Cameron, Kim, *Positive Leadership*.

————, *Positively Energizing Leadership*.

Chapman, Bob, and Raj Sisodia, *Everybody Matters*.

Collins, Jim, *Good to Great*.

Covey, Stephen, *The 7 Habits of Highly Effective People*.

Fry, Timothy, O.S.B., *The Rule of St. Benedict*.

Galbraith, Craig, and Oliver Galbraith III, *The Benedictine Rule for Leadership*.

Goldsmith, Marshall, *What Got You Here Won't Get You There*.

Gordon, Jon, *The Power of Positive Leadership*.

Grant, Adam, *Think Again*.

Havard, Alexandre, *Created for Greatness.*

———, *The Virtuous Leader.*

Jeanne, Buckeye, Kenneth Goodpaster, T. Dean Maines, and Michael Naughton, *Respect in Action.*

Kaczor, Christopher, *The Gospel of Happiness.*

Kotter, John, *Leading Change.*

Lyubomirsky, Dr. Sonya, *The How of Happiness.*

Novak, Michael, *Business as a Calling.*

Peters, Tom, *Re-Imagine.*

Pink, Daniel, *Drive.*

Quinn, Robert, *Deep Change.*

Quinn, Robert, and Anjan Thakor, *The Economics of Higher Purpose.*

Rath, Tom, *Strengths Based Leadership.*

Rey, Carlos, Miquel Bastons, et al., *Purpose Driven Organizations.*

Ries, Eric, *Lean Startup.*

Rock, Michael, *St. Benedict's Guide to Improving Your Work Life.*

Seligman, Dr. Martin, *Flourish.*

Sinek, Simon, *Start with Why.*

———, *The Infinite Game.*

Skrabec, Quentin, *St. Benedict's Rule for Business Success.*

Turak, August, *Business Secrets of the Trappist Monks.*

Wolf, Notker, and Enrica Rosanna, *The Art of Leadership.*

Wong, Kenman and Scott Rae, *Business for the Common Good.*

About the Author

> My purpose is to teach, guide and
> inspire people so that they can
> flourish in their work and lives.

Mike Ferrell is an entrepreneur, certified executive coach, consultant and author, and works with businesses, organizations and institutions helping them in the areas of leadership, innovation, sales development and strategic planning. He has over thirty years of experience working with small businesses, Fortune 500 corporations, the United States military and non-profit organizations. Mike has extensive experience in the financial services industry and has had over twenty-five hundred advisors and managers go through his training, development and coaching programs. He has been involved in fourteen different start-up companies and has worked with businesses in thirty-seven different industries.

He currently serves Mount Marty University as the Director of Professional Development for the Benedictine

Leadership Institute developing and delivering programs on leadership and innovation for organizations, municipalities and churches. He is also the founder and partner of Principled Flourishing Group.

Mike is a graduate of The University of St. Thomas and St. John Vianney Seminary in St. Paul, Minnesota. Mike is trained in Gallup StrengthsFinder, Values in Action Inventory, Virtuous Leadership and has a certificate in Positive Psychology. Mike lives with his wife Anne in Sioux Falls, South Dakota. Mike is also a Benedictine Oblate.

To learn more about Mike's work and access additional resources visit www.principledflourishing.com.